Oh Ron,

I'm so happy we're on this journey. I'll be so pleased when you're signing my copy of your book ♡

Angela
2/18/13

# Salt
## in the
## Sugar Bowl

### A Novella by
### Angela Belcher Epps

Mint Hill Books
Main Street Rag Publishing Company
Charlotte, North Carolina

Copyright © 2013 Angela Belcher Epps
Cover art by M. Scott Douglass

Acknowledgments:

> Earlier versions of "Sophia" and "Hunter" appeared in *Obsidian: Literature in the African Diaspora*.

Library of Congress Control Number: 2012953880

ISBN: 978-1-59948-402-0

Produced in the United States of America

Mint Hill Books
PO Box 690100
Charlotte, NC 28227
www.MainStreetRag.com

*To my mother, Odessa,
whose salt-of-the-earth wisdom
is a comfort to us all*

## SPECIAL THANKS

Thank you Bridget Connolly for fanning the flame that became this novella. Thank you Stephanie McIntyre for reading with eagle eyes and discussing the chapters whenever I asked. Thank you Beth Browne for ideas and encouragement along the publication journey. Thank you Yasirah Vanessah for raising my technological literacy. And thank you Bernard for having faith in me as a writing warrior.

# CONTENTS

Sophia—1984 . . . . . . . . . . . . . 1

Hunter—1992 . . . . . . . . . . . . . 14

Carlene—1992 . . . . . . . . . . . . . 20

Eva—1997 . . . . . . . . . . . . . . 46

Cook and Marina—2004 . . . . . . . . . . 56

Kurt—2008 . . . . . . . . . . . . . . 75

Boyd and Lisa—2010 . . . . . . . . . . . 97

## SOPHIA—1984

Sophia's strong, waitress legs felt thin and weak; it had been two days since she'd had so much as a cracker. And because she knew now, firsthand, that she was weak in all the ways a person shouldn't be. She bumped back and forth down the aisle, holding onto the backrests of the Coastline Express toward an empty seat. Maybe the bus would have a freak accident with her as the only fatality. Have it known that Sophia Sawyer died on a bus, unexpectedly, thirty-five miles from her home. Death was palatable. They could put it in the obituary section, and her people could have a good cry, then put a period at the end of her life and move on. There was nothing palatable about a woman leaving six children behind in Haden, N.C. on a balmy April morning—with no intention of ever looking back.

As the flat, black fields of eastern North Carolina gave way to thick swamp foliage, Sophia would not look. She passed the only places she'd ever known in her 39 years with her eyes covered by her long, tan hands squeezing against a headache, or more of a brain ache, that felt like a sharpened hatchet hacking away at her skull. Before she knew it, she had let out an animal moan. She had proven, as clear as wedding crystal, that she was not the woman anybody thought she was—including herself.

The only thing she knew about this new self was that she would go to Norington. She could make a living there. Anybody could who didn't mind work. In Norington, she could live off the profits left by a steady stream of tourists. People who had it easy enough to lie on beach chairs, and swim in indoor pools, and ride bikes up and down the strip. With no thought at all, she could hand people towels, change beds, load and unload mountains of soiled and clean linen, serve food and drinks. Any of that worked for her. It was her own life that she had no more stomach for.

Just after 2 p.m. she arrived and grabbed her cylindrical duffel bag from the sidewalk where the driver had slung it. The crowd cleared, and Sophia sat on the side of the building in a faded plastic chair. A dozen yards away, a man dozed, his chin tucked fowl-like onto his chest. A woman, barefoot with sun-streaked hair, sat on the curb smoking. Sophia sat, afraid to move. She now understood how a person could walk into a brick wall and slam her head against it over and over to escape from the pain happening inside it. Sophia walked slowly across the platform toward a wooden structure called The Convenience Mart. "A pack of Camels," she ordered. The no nonsense brand her grandfather had smoked. Back outside, she lit the cigarette and held the smoke in against a cough. She was forced to breathe to keep from choking. Sophia's thoughts settled for the first time since the storm had arrived at her door three days before.

That storm had blasted through her life when a social worker, a very young Miss Dalton, knocked on her front door. Miss Dalton had a baby in her arm and a little boy by the hand. Sophia's first instinct was to reach for the baby girl because Miss Dalton carried the baby like a bag of groceries that was seconds away from slipping to the ground. But in a flash of clear thinking and with 20/20 eagle eyes, Sophia glanced down and recognized the double dimple on the little boy's chin. And like that, she knew they were her husband's children. And that knocked the wind out of her, and her head started spinning and didn't ever stop.

Then Miss Dalton said, "Excuse me, m'am, but I was sent to bring these children to your home because their mother is very sick. Is Mr. Sawyer home yet?"

Sophia shook her head. She squinted.

"Their mother, Ms. Portia Basnight, has suffered a breakdown. We're not sure what it is. The neighbors called it a fit."

Sophia could only stare. She wanted to slam the door and go back several years in time, and be living at some other address without this husband and this life.

"They took her to the facility in Goldsboro. The neighbors told us Mr. Sawyer is their father, so is he home?"

Sophia shook her head.

Miss Dalton shifted the baby. "He probably will be soon because my supervisor called his job and said there was an urgent matter, and was he able to meet us at his home."

Sophia ran her hands through a thick mass of curls. She was still in her tight black pants and white three-button rayon shirt—the uniform from waiting tables from breakfast through the late lunch. She wanted a shower. She wanted a cup of coffee. She wanted thirty minutes off her feet before she had to start dinner, and before her children came home. She wanted this not to be happening at her front door.

"Can I bring them in to wait?" Miss Dalton asked. "My arm feels like it's breaking."

Sophia could not speak. She stepped aside.

Sophia left them there and walked through her house. As she went in and out of the rooms—three bedrooms, each with its dingy bedspreads and sagging curtains, Sophia saw nothing but disappointment. A whole 20 years amounted to next to nothing. Where were the blinders she had put on everyday to be a human glue gun? Without them, she saw nothing to hold together. Walls unpainted for the whole time they'd lived in this perfectly square ranch house too tight for anybody to grow in any direction. The floors creaking under cheap carpet the color of dirt. What the hell color had it been in the first place? Her anger, confusion, and tension crawled into every nerve and cell; any touch of sweetness that she felt about her life finally gave way to a brine at the back of her throat and brewing behind her eyes.

Sophia edged to the living room when she heard Hunter's key slip into the door. The baby slept in the social worker's arms, and the boy sat playing with his fingers. Hunter, slick with sweat and oil, stepped into the room. The boy sprang up and ran, screaming, "Daddy!" Hunter reached down and scooped him up. "Hey, boy!" Then, as if remembering his whereabouts, his eyes surveyed the room. Sophia held his gaze for a mere second before going to the back of the house. This wasn't going to be her business.

That evening not one angry word passed her lips, not a tear dropped. She paid no attention to the two babies. Her children accepted them like surprise pets—examining them, picking them up, rubbing them, probably wondering if they would keep them. Sophia and Hunter's eyes did not meet, and he offered no words of explanation or apology. Nearing bedtime, he'd said, "I'll sleep out here with them till we figure out what to do." Sophia nodded. She ignored the *we*. This definitely was not going to be her business.

And she wasn't going to make it a sad and long-suffering situation to get through. Haden was a small town, no more than 2,500 people. And it was not her home, and she did not have a sprawling nest of relatives to make it worth her while to stay in a place she probably should have left years ago. These thoughts came throughout the evening and night without invitation. She didn't set the intention to leave. But her mind would not, absolutely refused to, look in the direction of living with this backhanded slap.

Maybe Sophia should have left when it dawned on her that her husband didn't really want her—even though he seemed to try. Sophia accepted this fact, like a little *P.S. I don't love you* that would have been written at the bottom of a letter. She let it rest at the back of her mind like a cancer seemingly in remission, but not declared gone. She never blamed him for it, and always believed the problem was hers. And it was nothing she ever tried to explain to anyone else because they naturally saw him as the wrongdoer. Because Hunter was the kind to run with other women—not so openly that Sophia came across anything concrete. But he came and went often—in a way that kept his wife from wanting to ask questions. And his name might crop up in a conversation, then suddenly be dismissed because the speaker realized it was headed down a wrong path.

But Sophia blamed herself because her mother had taught her pretense as if it was some wonderful skill—without thinking through what happened after the false advertising. Sophia had met Hunter after high school, when she was cashiering at the A&P. Hunter was a temporary worker at Hofneister Mill, and didn't know much of anything about Maxton County. He met Sophia at the time her mother, Devora Douglas, was pushing Sophia to take herself up a notch. Devora cut out pictures from magazines and bought make up. She set up and paid for Friday evening hairdresser appointments for her daughter, and she coaxed Sophia to spend entire paychecks on dresses that lifted her average-sized breasts and cinched her nonexistent waist. It was 1964, and while most Maxton County women were still modest in their knee-length shirtwaists, Devora's magazines were showing dresses way up on the thigh. So it didn't matter how much of a waist her daughter didn't have when a dress was that short.

Devora knew how to reel in a lonely man; she had reeled in plenty and married three of them. She nudged Sophia to invite Hunter to dinner, and Devora credited Sophia with the production. Hunter Sawyer was blind-sided by the glamorized Sophia among the drab selection in Maxton County. In less than six months they were married at the Hope and Savior Baptist Church with a feast for seventy-five in the church dining room. Both Sophia and Devora were overwhelmed by the 6'2", good-looking, hard-working Hunter. Sophia remembered her mother pinching her cheek and winking on the receiving line after the wedding. She didn't wink back.

Sophia was 19, and marriage was fine for the first few months because she and Hunter lived with Devora while he finished out his contract. Sophia and Devora hadn't thought much about what to do once she moved to her own house in Haden and couldn't match colors, or season a chicken, or hem her dresses, or apply false eyelashes on her own.

In no time, Hunter was asking why he kept getting strangled with too much vinegar. Then Sophia gave birth to their first child, Boyd, and she had no paycheck coming in. She saw how Hunter looked sideways at her hair sprouting wild and wooly with no beautician to work magic. To make it worse, Devora died from a massive, after-dinner heart attack shortly before the birth of their second child, Eva. The baby weight clung, and there was no Devora coaching about what to eat and not eat, and gone were the short, form-fitting dresses to camouflage her new, maternal shape.

To say Hunter was disappointed didn't do it justice. His discontent was like a force field between them. There were no more long, sucking kisses. No unexpected grabbing and rubbing. Sophia didn't have any tricks up her sleeve, and there was no money to create Devora's mirages. Hunter had brought home the little prize on the middle shelf instead of the big, top shelf, glossy one he'd been promised. They couldn't ever seem to get beyond it. Sophia silently watched her failures and questioned everything about herself. She hadn't been smart in school, but something told her she should have been, would have been if things had been different. But different how? Born in another town? Born to another mother who bought books instead of perfume? Born to two parents instead of one? She didn't know. But being married, having two babies, and running a house, who had time to think about intelligence? After a while, being in the house with babies all day made her want to slither out of her skin, so to save her mind and make some extra cash, Sophia got a job at Kilpatricks' Grill and Bakery, and she didn't think much at all. The years just ticked by.

With each child born, Hunter had pulled further back. He got tighter with his money. If they went somewhere, he walked on ahead, not bothering to help her get their children in and out of the car. The few places they went weren't much fun for either of them. So they went fewer and fewer places together. From the corner of her eyes, Sophia watched her family. Watching everything became her habit. She couldn't control much of anything that Hunter or the children did when they were out of sight, but at least she could see what was happening on her watch. Maybe that's why Miss Dalton and the two children took all the starch from her spine, and knocked her back to her own Square One. She hadn't seen that coming at all.

It was Carlene, their second-to-last child, that seemed the deal breaker. Neither Sophia nor Hunt intended to make another baby, but mistakes did happen. Sex was like an accident between them—a random rollover in the bed at just the right moment, and it happened. Not often, and neither of them told themselves cozy stories about it meaning more than that. During that pregnancy their home took on a darkness—like the sky of an approaching storm. There was more quiet, more exiting and empty rooms; and there were more excuses for everybody to be anywhere but at home. The children found friends that welcomed one more at the dinner table, or who had room in their cars. Hunter worked more and more overtime, but brought home less and less money. Sophia reserved her brightest smiles and softest words for the customers at the grill because the air within their home tolerated no such nonsense. She kept one foot in front of the other, doing what she could for her children, hoping the storm would ultimately pass them by. She watched and waited. It never passed. It just worsened with the last child, Kurt, who was conceived with the same kind of bumping in the night.

Hunt slept in the living room on a pallet with his two outside children for the second night. Sophia had not slept more than an hour, maybe two, since the children had come. Going to the kitchen for a drink, she glanced into the living room and saw Hunt curled around the children on the pallet. His arm fell across the boy who was pressed against his stomach. The baby was tucked in a ball, inches from Hunter's head. But behind Hunter, like a barnacle, was their own four-year-old, Kurt. Sophia paused and watched the peace, heard the steady breathing of Hunt with his children—including her own baby. And what she saw was love. She didn't see it often, but there it was—stronger than the cheating and lying and disappointment and confusion. Love is what Sophia noticed, and once she had drank down two tall glasses of tap water, she got the notion to pack her bags.

While Hunter sometimes seemed to be her own personal demon, Sophia knew he would have been a much better husband to somebody else. Over the years, Sophia witnessed over and over how much nicer Hunt was to their children when she wasn't around. Maybe then he saw less of her and more of himself in them. Behind her back, he gave them extra money, told jokes and laughed at theirs. She saw these things from the kitchen window, from down the hall, across the yard, through the rearview mirror. He never let

Sophia witness his soft side. But she'd seen him teach Boyd to ride a bike. She'd seen him bend to tie their shoes. She'd overheard Hunt ask how much money they needed for the school dance, for the fair or school trip, for some small thing Sophia didn't even know he was aware of. Yes, it was her he couldn't love.

Now Hunter's secret family was out of the bag. Sophia speculated. Hunt had every reason to take his chances with the other woman. A woman who had fits and babies that he loved. Sophia's instincts, her years of watching and wondering, told her to go. Get out of the picture so this man would not pick up and leave the six children he had fathered with a wife he didn't love. She pulled the strings of the duffel bag closed. What she could offer her children was worth next to nothing. Minimum wages and tips. Of course there was love, but God, Sophia thought, sometimes a mother's love was like a curse. Cruel as it sounded, when her guard was down and she was enjoying a cup of coffee, Sophia often thought Devora had done an awful thing. A mother could send all the wrong messages, and if the child wasn't smart enough to make her way out of the smoke and mirrors, she could end up in the exact places she didn't need to be. Maybe Sophia was the same kind of damaging mother, with all the doubting and watching, with too little action. Hunt had both love and money, and he probably didn't waste so much time wondering what to do. Maybe he could just make up his mind and do right by them all— whatever that was.

On the way home from Kilpatricks on the third day, Sophia took a twenty-five mile detour and bought a bus ticket. After that, she had 172 dollars in her purse, and a closed bank account. Driving home in her 1976 Gran Torino she turned on the radio to drown out the noise blaring in her brain. The second song that played was announced as *Hungry Heart*. She didn't know who it was by, but she heard that first line and turned it up as loud as she could. A man was singing about having a wife and kids in Baltimore. He was going out for a ride and he wasn't coming back. It was a sign from God, Sophia thought.

That night Sophia awakened Eva, her oldest girl. Her two younger girls slept in a double bed across the room. She crawled into the single bed and lay down beside her 16-year-old daughter. Eva jumped, shocked by the frizzy head so near her face. "Shhh. It's Mom." It wasn't like Sophia to get so close. She was not the touchy, soothing mother. But she wanted to remember this for what it was—the last time she'd touch her daughter. Even knowing it, it didn't seem possible, and Sophia said the words and ran her finger along Eva's hairline as if acting in a play. "I'm leaving your daddy," she said.

Eva's response was to cry. Her very next breath was a whining sob from deep in her chest.

"I know. I know it may be wrong. I know it's going to hurt everybody." It was the first time there was any mention of any of it to anybody. Sophia's friends were arms-length women. They joked and ate lunch together, and now and then shared some news, but there was nobody Sophia ever poured out her heart to.

"What? Where are you going?"

"I can't say where I'm going yet." She pressed Eva's head onto her shoulder "Don't say anything. Just listen. I think this is the only thing to do."

"When are you coming back?" Eva sat up. "Are you leaving because of his kids?"

"I'm leaving because I think things will get a lot worse for everybody as long as I'm here." She had to steel herself to say the next part. "Eva, I'm not coming back."

"That's crazy. Why are you saying this?" Eva, true to form as the oldest girl, whispered to keep from waking the others. "You can't leave and not come back. You're just crazy 'cause of Natalie and Charles. Mom, you should just go to bed."

"Listen. Your daddy will be better to you in the long run than I will. I love you, but I don't have anything to give you. I don't know what will happen with these new children, but there's two things I don't want to happen. I don't want to sit here and watch him love these new ones while he shortchanges my children to spite me. And I don't want him to leave us all here while he moves to wherever their mother is to be their family while we make ends meet on the little bit I bring in. Those are two things that I'm not going to let happen. The only way I have any control, any power in this, is if I go."

"If he leaves us here, it's okay. He's still in Haden. We can see him. I won't like it, but we can see him. You can't just go and not come back. Just take us with you. That's what people do." Eva's body heaved against Sophia.

Sophia held Eva, rubbed her hands briskly up and down her back, and whispered over her shoulder. "Eva, listen."

"I can't."

"You have to listen." Sophia took in enough air to keep from losing it. She talked slow enough to keep the tears at bay. Her body trembled with the tension; her jaws were tight; she fought against dizziness. "You're going to have to do so much with me gone."

And Sophia explained to an unwilling daughter that her childhood was over. She was the one who had to insist, and Sophia used the word *insist*, that her father take her grocery shopping on Fridays. And she was to insist that he give her enough cash to buy detergent and school clothes and enough for sanitary pads and tampons and whatever else they needed. Eva listened with swollen eyes; she seemed to shrink in size and courage. Sophia shook her shoulders. "Trust me, Eva. I know this is the right thing to do." Sophia said it with her mother's voice. "Trust me. It's me he doesn't want to give his money to. You're his first daughter, and you're special to him. I see it in his eyes all the time. It's me he doesn't love. He won't let you children go without.

Especially if you don't have your mother. So I know it's wrong to put this on you, but do not wake up and tell your father what I'm telling you, because I thought this out as far as I can, and it's the only thing that works. Trust me."

Sophia knew that was the truth. She repeated it enough times for Eva to remember, and to remember it herself. There was no way of convincing. It just had to be said. So Sophia went around the girls' room and then the boys' room kissing them lightly enough for them to sleep through it. She put her duffel bag in the trunk, then came back inside and went back to bed. She slept for the first time in days.

When she drove off to work the next morning, she didn't look back. When she finished her shift, Sophia drove her car to the train station twenty miles away and left it there. She walked two and a half miles alongside the two-lane highway, in the gravel, until she reached the small, grimy Hedham Hotel in Leesville where the bus made its pickup at 11:15 every morning. She paid the $29 plus tax for a room, and when the bus pulled in the next morning, Sophia was the only one to board.

A boy and his mother got off the evening bus. Still Sophia sat in the chair growing stiff and a little dizzy from the Camels. She had left, but there was nowhere she had to be. She was caught in the mental space of thinking but not thinking—where everything was going on underneath, and none of it was registering. While the mother retrieved the bags from the side of the bus, the boy hopped around trying to get Sophia's attention. His movements, so wild and close to her, roused Sophia and she caught herself. *I can't just sit here.* She'd been in the same spot for hours. She felt gone to the very core of her bones. This boy was a sudden reminder that her whole adult life was made up of minutes and hours spent feeding, tending, wiping, and chastising her children. With the transaction of money for ticket, it was all over. She had no life. She had to make one, because she realized people did end up sitting on benches smoking cigarettes for the rest of their lives.

    Sophia thought of her oldest boy, Boyd. He was already gone and living his own life. Chances were she'd never see him again. People were bound to say, "She'll make it back someday. She'll probably come to her senses and come back to all these children." But Sophia already knew she wouldn't. Because already, she couldn't even meet the small boy's eyes.

    Sophia stood straight and stretched. She wore a long denim skirt and a tee-shirt. Everything was behind her. She looked at the sidewalk trying to latch onto a thought to move her away from this chair on the side of a building. *What color do you like?* Sophia whispered to herself. *What's your favorite color?* She prodded. *Blue*, she finally answered. Okay. Blue. Sophia picked up her bag and walked slowly in the direction of the first pastel blue motel.

# HUNTER–1992

Hunter Sawyer sat at the table with a nearly scalding cup of coffee. He liked it black because he liked it hot—and if he added even a drop of sugar or a drip of milk, it was ruined. And Hunter needed as much heat as he could get. These days, he was always cold. Now he sat at his sister Edna's kitchen table with a mug of coffee so hot that his hands were uncomfortable. He felt at peace for the first time in weeks.

Edna was Hunter's favorite sister. There were five Sawyer siblings. Hunt was right in the middle—the one Edna said would have been overlooked altogether if not for her. Although she was seven years younger than he was, she was known to have more common sense than the rest of them—parents included; so she was the one Hunt trusted the most.

And Edna knew how to put things together so they looked so nice—like no other woman Hunt had ever known. His heavy heart was finally made lighter with the strong coffee and bakery bread Edna sat on the table between them. His heart needed the warmth of this afternoon because he'd been sleepless and aimless for the better part of three weeks. His doctor had confirmed cancer. He couldn't quite call him his doctor because it was only the second time he'd seen the man. It took nine weeks before his appointment rolled around. It pissed Hunt off that he could have been dead by the time they worked him in. The first visit had warranted blood tests and a chest x-ray. The follow-up delivered the diagnosis.

"Lung cancer, Stage 4," the doctor said.

When Hunt left the doctor's office, he was stunned. Like a mechanic had said he needed a new transmission at a time when he only had ten dollars to his name. He'd walked out strong, straight, and dry-eyed, but bewildered. What disturbed Hunt the most was he wanted a cigarette more than anything in the world, but sure as shit, if he lit up and inhaled more than twice, he would cough up blood. There was no more need to work his way down the aisle testing different cough syrups, drink spoons full of vinegar and honey, or rub Vicks on his chest. The options were now chemotherapy and radiation—with no guarantee that either one would buy much time.

The first week he found out, Hunt fixated on how little time he'd spent doing things he wanted to do. Did most people feel like that? The closest he and his buddies got to the good life was having a couple—or six or seven. Hanging at the liquor houses when the drinks went down easy and the pockets could keep them coming. So to keep his pockets lined, seemed like he had worked from dark to dark most of the days of his life. Because part of being a man meant having enough money left to let off some of the pressure. Cause pressure kept steadily building up, and money in the pockets was like a release valve.

There had been a time when he thought women could release the pressure, but he was young then. Real young. Back when he bought a brand new GTO and his head turned on its own axle without any input from his brain. And his small head, as they called it, rose up and took notice whenever it got a notion. So back then, there wasn't much pressure, and he didn't do much thinking. But that's how he wound up married and sort of bowled over with surprise—sort of like he'd come out of a coma and found his life changed forever. Right about that time he learned women had the upper hand, always had and always would, as far as he could see. While he was working and counting his money, women were writing a whole movie script that he was co-starring in without even knowing it. And God help him, he never got his lines right. Most of the time he hadn't even been interested in learning his lines. Now he knew pressure didn't really get released. It built up and built up—filling up all the spaces he wasn't aware of until a strange doctor found it and named it cancer.

Hunt wondered if he should tell Edna. He needed his sister right about now, but he needed her strong and cocky the way she was. She was like a girl/woman. That's how he thought of her. She lived in the city limits with her husband with a slip of backyard just big enough for a barbecue and a picnic table. Now he looked out her back window thinking how simple her life was. She'd made it that way. She was 42 to his 49, and nobody had managed to wear her out. So it was always good to be near Edna, because life hadn't done anything that tore her down for good. He hated he was here to complicate it.

Hunt broke the silence. "If anything happens to me, would you take Kurt and Carlene till they finish school? And Carlene's baby too. Jesus Christ. I know it's a lot."

"Where are you going? You're not planning to up and leave, are you? It's been done before." Edna only half-smiled.

He cleared his throat. "Just if anything happens. You never know. They've been through enough already."

"What about Nat and Charlie?"

"Well their grandmother's always got room for them. They're over there half the time anyhow. It's Sophia's kids need the most mothering, being so young when she left them. If it wasn't for you, wouldn't be no woman in their lives at all."

"True. I'd take them. But I'm only agreeing to make you feel good. Nothing's happening to you."

"You just never know. I appreciate it. But you know Carlene is wild as weeds right now. I don't want to sell you a lemon."

"Yeah well. I know who she is. Who's her daddy?"

"Yeah well. You get what you get."

"Just hang in there, Hunt. I know it gets hard, but you're almost done. Your hair's still thick and black. Your nest will be empty one of these days. You can start a whole new life in a few years. And imagine, starting a life with more sense this time." She sipped her coffee, looked straight at him with decades of knowing traveling between them. "But if anything happened to you, of course I'd take them. And I know what I'd be getting."

Hunt craved a cigarette so bad that he lifted himself off the seat for no reason. Then he sat back down. Then he got back up and refilled his coffee. Nobody thinks they're going to die at 49. Especially not a healthy somebody still working 8 to 5 in a welding plant—then doing pick-up jobs on the side. Not somebody who got to work 20 minutes early everyday to make the first pot of break room coffee in time for a cup and a cigarette in the smoke hut with the six buddies he'd worked with for 22 years. Not somebody with the gumption to uphold eight healthy kids when their mothers, God help them, were weak as worms. Many's the day he'd walked across the parking lot or down some school hallway to take care of some problem or other, and he asked himself out loud, *How the hell did I get to be mother and father to so many kids?*

"It's a sorrowful mystery," Edna always said. "One that will never be answered."

"For the record," Hunt said, as if he'd never said it before. "I believe with every drop of blood in my body that

Sophia Douglas, and notice I have taken back my name from that creature, was a piece of worthless shit for leaving her own children to be raised by the likes of me. I hope to God, wherever she is, that she is not carrying my name with her after she proved how much she thought of the children I gave her."

"Yeah. But you made it a little hard for her, don't you think?"

"I take some blame. Of course. I'm not stupid."

"Remember that. I mean, two kids? In Haden? A town a good pitcher could throw a ball half way through? I mean you can blame her, but then again, you can't blame her."

"But for me to be all they had? Wouldn't any decent mother want better for her children?"

They'd had this conversation a hundred times. Sometimes he needed to get some of it off his chest. It was like Edna had a way of knowing. She'd call him up early in the morning, or on the job, or late in the evening, and say, "Meet me," like they lived in some city instead of 12 minutes away from each other. So they would pull up to the Dairy Barn, or Kilpatricks, or Tall Man's, or to a liquor house, and drink coffee, sweet tea, beer, a milkshake or whatever was offered. Maybe a sister was the real release valve.

"Can we sit out back?" Hunt asked, already standing. They moved to the porch after refilling their cups. The pot was nearly empty. "You know what I regret the most, Ed? I'd walk into my own house, and the whole place was screaming for a woman. And damned if I could bring one home."

But that didn't matter now. People had a way of putting death and fantasies together: If you had a month to live, what would you do? Now Hunt knew. There was nothing different. He still had to pay the bills and put food on the table, so he would work until he couldn't get up in the morning or make it through the day. There was no money stashed in a bank account to do something he always wanted. So there had been no big fantasies. This was it. This was all there was.

Hunt looked up through the dense pines lining Edna's yard. There was so much light in the sky, but so little leaked through the needles. He leaned back and stared for quite a while. Quiet. Relaxed. And it dawned on him, in the stingy sun in Edna's eastern exposure at 4 p.m. The only love he had ever been certain of was that he had for his sister and his children. All eight of his children. He could name them all in order in his sleep and spell their first names backwards. He'd done it with all of them when they were young. At that moment, he knew exactly how old each one was down to the day. He sat there and worked it out in his mind. He would forgive any one of them for anything they had ever done or ever would do. He couldn't say the same for the women. He wouldn't trust any one of them any further than he could through her. And they probably felt the same about him. And rightly so. And with that thought, he felt better. "Let's have a shot," he said to Edna.

"What kind? I got scotch, vodka, a little tequila." She drew out the tequila extra long.

"Let's go for the tequila."

So they had a couple of shots, and soon they were laughing about nothing, and later still, they threw some hotdogs on the hand-built grill Edna's husband, Gabe, kept ready to fire up.

Before he left, Hunt hugged Edna tight and said with a light spirit, "There's nothing like a sister." He kissed her firmly on the jaw. That evening, when he got into his 1984 Ford F-150, he felt like he had been wrapped in a good-quality electric blanket. He was able to hold onto that warmth until the moment of his death two weeks later.

## CARLENE—1992

Carlene got her driver's license four months ago, but she kept it in her sock and underwear drawer. She could have driven Hunt's truck if she wanted, but she loved her bike. When she was 13, she'd weighed 210 pounds. Now she was 16 and weighed 112. Not because she dieted, but because she rode her bike wherever she could. When the last of her older sisters left home, and she became the oldest, Carlene went as far away from the house as often as she could. A year ago, she'd bought an odometer, and the furthest she'd ever ridden was 52 miles. 104 miles round trip. Riding taught her to be alone, to keep her own company, to use her power however she could—by riding away, or riding faster, or running over or around something that got in her way.

It was the middle of the afternoon, and the sky had turned an eerie gray. She hoped a storm wasn't whipping around the corner. Carla, her seven-month-old baby was in the seat behind her, weighing down the back, slumped over with her fists in the air, squinting against the wind. She was a useless travel companion. Carlene didn't want to go home. Her house was filled with older siblings. Carlene's father, Hunt, was dead. There was no peace, no normal, just grief.

Carlene pedaled faster, but rain came in a sudden chilly sheet. She stood and pumped hard to cover more ground. Behind her, Carla was shaking her head, batting her face, sucking in her breath in uneven pants—too stunned to cry.

It had been three days since Hunt died. In four days, after the funeral was over and the siblings had gone back to their lives, she, Baby Carla, and her younger brother, Kurt, would go to live with Aunt Edna. The two youngest half-siblings—Natalie and Charles, had been picked up by their maternal grandmother the same day Hunt died. Carlene was wired and tight; riding was the only release. Her freedom was slipping away. She forced her eyes to open wide in spite of the blinding rain. She rode faster.

Carlene wheeled the bicycle around the mud hole already forming on the rocked driveway. On the front and side doors of the square weathered ranch house—once bright yellow, now a sallow mustard, Aunt Edna had hung bright floral funeral wreaths. Carlene leaned the bike against the back porch noting how the rotting edges were soaked a soggy gray. Hunt had planned to replace those boards in a few weeks, once the spring rains slacked off. Carlene slung Baby Carla onto her hip and entered the kitchen—quietly, hoping they would go unnoticed. She and the baby dripped as if pulled from the river. Baby Carla buried her bald head in Carlene's shoulder against the possible onslaught of Sawyers filling the kitchen.

Eva, the oldest sister, came toward them. Carlene avoided Eva's eyes, maneuvered around her. She mumbled, "We're soaked." Eva thought she was the stand-in mother, but older is all she was. Already she had criticized Carlene's close-cropped hair, her dark, deep-set eyes rimmed in silver and charcoal, her lean face—browned and weathered from thousands of hours in the wind and sun.

Carlene dripped down the hallway into the back bedroom with Eva and Lisa following.

"Boyd says you're not planning to go to the funeral," Eva confronted her.

"No. I'm not," Carlene said.

"You have to go," Eva and Lisa said simultaneously.

"No I don't."

"Everybody will want to know where you are. They're going to wonder if you lost your mind, or died yourself. Look at you. What the hell have you been doing?" Eva looked her up and down. "You look like a grown woman. Remember you're still a child."

Carlene stripped the baby then removed her own jeans and tee-shirt. With a steel-laced expression, she said, "Eva please. Don't waste your time trying to change my mind." She glanced over at Lisa with the same warning. No way she was sitting through a funeral. Once the hearse took Hunt away, it was clear that the man on the stretcher was no longer her father. They pronounced him deceased as he sat upright on the couch. Carlene had slipped into the next room hoping his spirit still lingered in their home. She knelt in the corner. "Daddy, thank you for taking care of me. Thank you for never leaving me. Please Daddy, I don't know how, but send Momma back." She imagined her dad as a winged angel making visits in the night.

"Daddy would want us all together," Eva countered.

"Don't think for Daddy. If he needs somebody to think for him, I'll do it. I was here when he died. Alright?" Carlene struck a match and touched flame to cigarette. She hissed the smoke between clenched teeth. "He doesn't care whether I see him laid out in a coffin." She said it with finality.

"Blow the smoke away from the baby," was all Eva said.

Lisa, sitting cross-legged on the bed she'd slept in till she left home, said, "How about don't smoke around the baby. You guys are nuts. Your poor kids."

"Fuck you," Carlene and Eva said together.

All the siblings were rarely together. Too rare for anybody to slip in and make any assumptions at all. It smothered Carlene—having to be the young one after years of answering to nobody—except Hunt. Something bitter crawled around her stomach when her sisters took a tone with her.

    Carlene slipped the baby into a onesie, tiny cotton pants, and a sweatshirt. She pulled on dry jeans and a plain gray sweatshirt, no bra. She left the room and slipped out the side door. The sky was clear again by the time she strapped the baby in and mounted her black Schwinn. She could hear Hunt or one of his friends saying, "If you don't like the weather in North Carolina, just wait 15 minutes. It'll change." Her head would probably be filled with old men sayings forever. She was tired, and her legs ached as she bumped over the double railroad tracks, and down the streets toward town. Riding down the highway took concentration because the traffic was busy on Friday afternoons. But she felt spacey and exhausted. Seemed like she had been in nonstop motion since the rescue squad pulled off with her father's body.

    Carlene rode to Matthew's house. She had met him a year and a half ago at the fish market. Friday was always fish day, and Hunt sent her down to the river on Thursdays to buy fresh fish. On this particular day she stopped in Rowson's Fishery. Mr. Rowson's son, Matthew, was behind the counter. Carlene shoved her hands into the ice chips—examining fish after fish, laying the perfect ones on the scale.

    Matthew had approached the short, curvy girl with muscular legs, and long braids, "You know what you're doing?"

    Carlene was as good at picking fish as anybody. She'd watched Eva, then Lisa pick through them since she was 8 or 9. "Yeah. I've probably done it more than you. You work here now?"

    "Sometimes. It's my daddy's store. I'm Matthew."

    "Oh." Carlene kept picking through the porgies.

"So what's your name?"

"Carlene."

"So Carlene who knows so much about fish, do you know what to do with them after you've picked them out and taken 'em home?"

"Please. I can make a grown man cry if I fry a pan of fish." She said it without missing a beat, then looked at him from the corner of her eyes.

"It's been a long time since I cried. How about I dare you?"

"How 'bout I take you up on that. Tears will be running down your face." Words came to her from out of nowhere. Most times she didn't even know why she said what she did. But he asked for her number. And on Friday, after Hunt had eaten and gone out, and Natalie and Charles' grandma had taken them for the weekend, and Kurt was spending the night with a buddy, Carlene fried the five porgies she'd set aside for her and Matthew Rowson. She prided herself as the only real cook in the Sawyer family, and Carlene had sat eating proudly with the bold seventeen-year-old boy who'd driven up in a souped up Ford Maverick.

In spite of two older sisters, Carlene had had only one conversation about birth control in her entire life. Her friends had passed around condoms brought by a health class speaker from the county. After the presentation, the conversation was centered around *Have you ever done it?* and *Are you going to use them?* The questions circled among her friends—free of judgment or expectation. "No. Take mine," was all Carlene had said, passing hers to Lorna who absolutely was going to use them first chance she got. Carlene had no intention of having sex at 15. But three months later, she'd taken her pants off for Matthew without hesitation, and without the county woman's condoms.

Matthew was her first and only, and he was thrilled to have a virgin after a meal of fish, and a joint for dessert. "I think I am going to cry," he said smiling as he slipped into her on the sagging double bed.

"I told you so." Carlene did actually cry. She hadn't cared all that much for the sex—with the pain and the feeling of being slit open. But his large brown body holding her and stroking her, and his tender lips, still moist from her meal, kissing her and whispering to her, gave her a feeling that she most definitely wanted again. And again. And again.

Afterwards he'd lain sprawled on her bed, snoring. Carlene propped up on her elbow and watched him—thinking about sex for the first time. Wars started over it. What was it, the Trojan War that started over a woman? Something she'd learned in English class. Families dissolved over it. Women and men sat in prison because of it. Her mother left her father because of it. And while Matthew slept, she picked up his penis and examined the veins. She looked the snake-like tip in its face. She bent down and ran her fingertips lightly over the ridges of the leathery balls. And in the lamplight, with ample time to inspect way more than she probably should have, Carlene decided to fall in love with Matthew, so she could feel those arms and lips and legs—the whole of it, as often as she wanted. Nine months, nearly to the day, they had Baby Carla.

Carlene pulled around to the back of the Quonset hut and knocked on Matthew's window. The rain had started up again, and she and the baby were, again, soaked. Matthew worked the night shift at the fishery and slept most of the day. With the fog of sleep clinging to him, he let them in the side door close to his room. Tracy Chapman crooned low in the background and the close, dark room smelled of sleep breath and weed.

Matthew lifted the wet baby from Carlene's arms, looked in his daughter's face asking, "Nap after a long ride, little lady?" He walked directly to the bed, removed Baby Carla's clothing, dried her with an undershirt, and pulled a diaper from the nightstand. He handed Carlene a dry shirt. And inside of five minutes, he'd dropped back into sleep—pressing the baby in front of him.

Carlene pulled the plastic bear bottle from her knapsack. "Here you go." Baby Carla took it, lifted her leg, grabbed her toes. Carlene pulled off her own wet clothing, and buttoned herself into the soft cotton shirt. She settled on the floor, her back against the bed and, without looking, reached on the nightstand beside the lamp where she knew there'd be a joint. She lit it and smoked—pulling the strong weed deep into her lungs. She turned up the boom box and felt something close to sane.

Two days later, everybody tried, but nobody could make her go to the funeral. Eva tried the hardest. "Carlene," Eva said with tears running down her face. Her husband, Dan, stood holding her, pressing a paper towel to her cheeks. "Everybody in the family should be there." She'd already tried to get Boyd, the true oldest, to convince Carlene, but all he'd said was, "We can't force her."

Lisa, already dressed like a model in a lacy black dress and stiletto heels, rushed into the room and grabbed Carlene by the hand. "Listen. Nobody wants to go. Funerals aren't supposed to be fun. Do it for me. Come sit on the row so we can all be together. Carlene, please. It's not about just you. It's our whole family."

She snatched her hand back. "NO!" Carlene didn't mean to scream, but she did. "There is no whole family. Just stop! Cook's not here. Mom's not here. What whole family?"

Lisa threw up her hands, spun on her heels and clicked down the linoleum hallway. Then Aunt Edna, in a flowing black, peasant dress, practically crept into the room in rubber soles. "Come here." She opened her arms and brought Carlene into them. Carlene instantly thought of the years when Aunt Edna would pop in to do damage control. During the first couple of years after Sophia left, she'd swoop into their home on a Saturday or Sunday. Edna cleaned, then baked a chicken, or made a pot of stew. Kurt, Carlene, Nat, and Charlie would hold onto her dress and sit on her lap, and whenever she was in the right position, wrap their arms around her waist so she would massage their shoulders, or cradle their heads, or just squeeze back. She would put them to bed, but Carlene would stay awake as long as she could so Edna would sit by the side of the bed that much longer. And always, she cried when Edna left.

Carlene and Aunt Edna sat down on the bed she shared with Baby Carla. Carlene looked around the dingy bare walls as Aunt Edna held her hand. Old dried tacky spots where sisters had taped magazine pictures or photographs of their boyfriends made it even dingier.

Aunt Edna broke the silence. "The hearse and funeral car are leaving in about 45 minutes. Your sisters are going ballistic, but you're not budging are you?" Aunt Edna had made all the arrangements. Carlene didn't want Aunt Edna to take it personally. Like declining an invitation.

Carlene shook her head, a little bit ashamed.

"Can't take it?"

"No. I can't."

"I guess. You were here when he died. You're 16 years old. You've had enough."

Carlene nodded. "Did Boyd tell you Baby Carla was just sitting all quiet in Daddy's arms when he died?"

"Yeah. He did."

"Isn't that creepy? It's so weird that she was sitting so still. Even when I came in the room, she didn't like reach for me or anything. It's like she knew he was dead, and she was on her own. Weird."

"I'm so glad he had her with him. It's nice that he wasn't alone."

"That's what I think. Nat and Charlie were gone with their grandma. And I just went to get some stuff for dinner cause Daddy said he didn't feel like going out. There's a reason for everything." Another old man saying. Tears rolled down Carlene's face. "And he was so crazy about Baby Carla. He just ate her up. Sometimes he grabbed her and kissed her and nibbled her feet and her little legs and, I don't know, I'd feel good. Like everything was really okay. I think it was so cool he had her in his arms."

"She'll miss him."

They sat for a while—Carlene chipping silver blue polish from her short bitten nails, and Edna just breathing slow and steady, until Gabriel, Aunt Edna's short, handsome, Guatemalan husband poked his head in the door and said, "It's time to go." He nodded respectfully in Carlene's direction and patted his heart with his hand. It made Carlene cry all over again.

The family was lining up in the front of the house. It was a like a museum of black suits and dresses. Their neighbor was watching the babies on a pallet at her feet. Carlene scooped her baby up from among the gathering of small cousins. She strapped on their helmets and rode away.

As she rode, Carlene remembered one night when she was ten. She'd awakened way after midnight to the sound of voices and the smell of food. She was half asleep, but she felt an opening—a space of light and pure expectation. A Christmas morning feeling. She slipped out of bed, and tipped through the room—careful not to awaken the others. She glided across the floor, and for a few seconds she fantasized about telling all the others that Momma was back. Of waking them up and screaming. But then she caught a glimpse of Hunt at the table with a beer sweating in front of him. Sitting across from him was a stranger—a woman with her hair in a neat roll, a thin face, and sparkly lips. Carla stood there in a daze. They didn't see her standing yards away from them down the unlit hallway. It wasn't her mother. But Carlene took in the woman's slow and gentle movements, heard the watery clear voice cutting through smoky nighttime air; watched her pinky finger stiffen as she picked up a sandwich and clamped the full, shining lips down around it, then dab her lips with a napkin. Carlene had been hungry for the woman who looked like a mother sitting in their kitchen. She'd walked slowly into the kitchen and stood by the woman, leaned against her until the woman pulled her onto her lap. She put her head on the woman's shoulder. She would not meet her father's eye for fear he would send her back to bed. There was silence as they sat there. The woman picked up her drink and swallowed. Carlene inhaled deeply and melted against her. And the woman let her. Carlene never remembered how she got back to bed

Carlene knocked on the front door knowing Mrs. Rowson, Baby Carla's grandmother, would be home. She was always home when she wasn't working. It seemed like her life was spent preparing one continuous meal. "Come on in honey," she said.

"Hi." Carlene was used to dropping in.

"Hey Sweetie." Mrs. Rowson leaned her face to touch Baby Carla's cheeks. "Carlene, you alright? I know the funeral's today? I was going myself but Davie's sick."

Carlene nodded. Already Baby Carla's arms were reaching.

"Wait a minute, sweetie. Gramma's chopping onions."

Baby Carla immediately cried as if she understood the rejection.

Carlene shifted and bounced, bounced and shifted as Baby Carla shrieked and struggled. "I didn't bring her bottle." Carlene kept her eyes on Mrs. Rowson to gauge her response. Was she disgusted, amused, disappointed?

Mrs. Rowson's face was expressionless. She put down the onion, rinsed her hands, and reached high into a cabinet. "There's always a bottle in this house. Always. Hold on Sweetpea. We'll wash it out and put something in it, okay? Okay. Settle down, little miss." Mrs. Rowson balanced on tiptoes as her hand rummaged blindly on the top shelf. "See there. Look what Gramma's got for you."

"Wow. Like magic." Carlene shifted and bounced. She latched on to the small meaningless small talk Mrs. Rowson made as she scrubbed, then rinsed the old glass baby bottle. "Stop pulling. Gramma said wait a minute." And suddenly Carlene was crying along with the baby. She was surprised and embarrassed. "I don't know what I was thinking, not bringing her bottle. I just left the house. I wasn't thinking." Explaining made it worse. Her words were thick and slimy.

"Carlene." The woman dried her hands, reached down and took the baby. Her voice level, like she was making an official announcement. "Stop. Cut yourself some slack. You can't remember everything. You're a baby yourself. Your daddy just died. And you're not at the funeral. All that says to me you're in pretty bad shape."

Carlene cried harder. She wanted to sidle up to the soft woman smelling like onions as much as Baby Carla did. All the same, Mrs. Rowson would probably pay a huge price to go back 16 months and have her oldest son spend a particular weekend anywhere except with a just-turned 15-year-old girl at the Sawyer's house. Carlene was ashamed.

"Honey, you need some rest. Go in there and lay on the couch. Grab that throw off the lounger and put it over you. You've had a rough week. Lie down and take a nap."

Mrs. Rowson moved with the baby on her hip—maneuvering the Similac scoop, the container, the bottle, and the baby as if she was meant to perform such amazing feats.

Carlene walked to the woman and pressed her forehead against her back. Just for a moment. Mrs. Rowson stood still. Then Carlene followed the directions and went to do as she was told.

Carlene walked down the hall to the bathroom. She sat on the toilet for a long time—weak and more tired than she ever remembered feeling. Tears flowed like a rippling lake—easy and steady. She sat until there seemed to be no fluids left in her body. She wiped her face, avoided looking in the mirror, and went to the soft, rounded sofa with raised brown roses. Carlene pulled the throw from the armrest. As she lay down, she pulled it up under her chin. Her breath drew in as she experienced the snuggly, clean, fluffy fibers that smelled like some distant heaven. Warmth and tenderness were somehow woven into the very fabric of this thing. Carlene pressed herself to the back of the sofa, and settled the comforter under her nose and slept. She slept like it was another kind of bodily function that she was not acquainted with.

She slept through the sounds of silverware tinkling during a family dinner. Through the clanging of glass against metal against plastic in the running dishwasher. Through the muffled voices of Mr. and Mrs. Rowson as they watched television in the den, and through the controlled inside play of Matthew's little brothers and her own baby girl. Carlene awakened briefly when Matthew returned from work. He nudged her to come to his bed, certain his parents would overlook the rule on this once-in-a-lifetime devastating occasion. But Carlene did not want to go to his bed. She craved this spot at the heart of this home—clutching the glorious blanket, hearing every movement of every person, and inhaling the sweetness of this vacuumed and swept haven that had none of the grit and mildew that clung to every foot of her own home.

During the night, Mrs. Rowson asked, "You okay?" and touched Carlene's forehead.

Carlene could not find her voice. She felt a heat brewing at the backs of her eyes.

"You feel warm," Mrs. Rowson said. Seconds later, she handed Carlene tablets and a bottle of water. "Take these."

Carlene looked sleepily and silently into Mrs. Rowson's eyes and accepted the medicine. She was usually the one dispensing things to the younger ones. The heat increased beneath her eyes and worked its way through her body.

She tightened her grip on the throw, coiled her body into a human knot.

Carlene dreamt of Hunt. He was sitting on the back steps smoking a cigarette. She knew he was dead, and she watched him from the kitchen door. She didn't want to disturb him, but it took him a ridiculous amount of time to finish his smoke. She crept onto the porch to be closer to him. He did not turn around. When he'd smoked it down to the filter, Hunt flicked the butt into the grass, rose and began to walk down the path toward the road.

"Daddy," she called.

He didn't answer. Before he reached the street, he turned and threw his keys over his shoulders. Carlene reached out and caught them with both hands. That's when she awakened. Hunt's presence lingered. Carlene rubbed her cheek with the throw. He seemed so close. She thought about when Hunt brought her home after Baby Carla's birth. Carlene had wanted to stay in the hospital. The nurses were tucking her in, bringing her ice chips and presenting a menu to select three whole meals a day. But after three days, they sent her and the baby home. Carlene felt raw and petrified. Baby Carla was a pale red alien creature, the first infant she'd ever encountered. She didn't trust herself to handle the hideously skinny, wrinkled arms and legs, and a monstrous head. Her little pussy was purple and obscene. How could she take it home? Matthew was in and out with the same breezing in/got to go agenda he always had. At the hospital, he allowed Carla to be laid into his arms, and he sat nearly motionless until someone lifted the baby out again. He was of no comfort at all.

On the day of their release, Hunt showed up with Matthew to pick them up. As the young parents watched, Hunt placed the baby in the center of a pink flannel blanket. He tucked and folded it until Baby Carla was a neat, tight bundle. Hunt scooped her up and placed her in the carrier. He handed the carrier to Matthew, and he pushed Carlene's wheelchair quickly down the halls with the tote bags slung onto his shoulder.

Back at the house, Hunt sat on the side of Carlene's bed and changed Baby Carla's diaper. He did not flinch at the yellow mustard that had seeped from her creepy bottom. He rubbed A&D ointment all over it, and told Carlene and Matthew, "Use it every time, and she won't ever have diaper rash." He talked on and on about everything—how round Baby Carla's stomach was and how fat she would be, how to keep her head from falling back, to remember to feed her every three or four hours while he was out working, not to put her in the bed with her cause she might roll over and smother her. He left the light on and left for work—explaining how he would not call because they needed their sleep. In the morning, Hunt had put the baby in bed with him and said, "Go eat and take a shower. Eat the meat on the stove." And Carlene had—never worrying about anything at all. And from that day on Hunt would come in out of the blue and lift the baby from her arms saying, "Go have some fun," as if fun was a staple—like food and water. And it was. She was her father's child.

Carlene opened her eyes, just a fraction—enough to see the Rowson's weak pines swaying in the wind, a faint light of the rising sun filtering through them. Her baby would awaken soon, but that was okay. Baby Carla belonged to all of them. They claimed her and cared for her. Carlene closed her eyes, burrowed deep beneath the pink, white, and green fleece.

Carlene refused Mrs. Rowson's offer of a glass of juice before she went off to work the next morning. Carlene was holding onto her fever like a life preserver. She slept through the comings and goings of the Rowsons' school and workday. The muted interactions between Baby Carla and Matthew as he fed and bathed and changed his daughter in lieu of getting his daytime sleep were like whispers on the wind.

Late—after everyone had returned home, a hand shook Carlene awake. This was not the soft touch of Mrs. Rowson, and it was definitely not Matthew. It was Boyd's rough hand laid on her shoulders. She frowned.

"I hear you got sick. We were worried about you." He sat with his bulky body perched on the edge of the sofa.

There was nothing to say. She did not want to go with him, but this was not her home. Silent tears flowed as she scanned the area for her belongings. Her backpack and her shoes stood neatly at the end of the sofa. She put on her sneakers, then quickly, rolled the throw into a snug bundle and stuffed it into her backpack.

"Honey, why don't you leave Carla here with us for a couple of days. Take some time to get yourself better. I'll get her to daycare and Matt'll pick her up. We have plenty of her stuff here. That be okay?"

Carlene nodded. She walked closer to Mrs. Rowson and hugged her. Mrs. Rowson put one hand on Carlene's head and pressed it to her shoulder, patted her back with the other. One racking sob escaped from Carlene, and her shoulders pulsated with the force of the dark despair she felt leaving this house—with no place in front of her that she wanted to be.

Boyd put his arm around her when Mrs. Rowson released her with her own eyes glistening with sympathy.

Carlene's bicycle was in the back of Boyd's truck. He opened the door for her, held her backpack as she climbed in. She had not said a word. The tears eased as they made their way up Highway 33—past American VideoPlex, Foodland, and several industrial farms. They rode through town with shadow people moving to and from their cars. Boyd broke the silence when they went over the Blockstown Bridge—a few minutes from the house. "We really were worried. Kurt said you'd be there, and of course we missed you at the funeral. But I understand. Really I do."

Carlene willed herself to nod—to acknowledge him. It wasn't his fault.

"I wished you had called. We would've picked you up yesterday. We love you. We were worried."

She nodded again.

"Now that Daddy's gone, you have to call us. Let us know what you need. Okay?"

She shook her head, wanting to tell the truth to them. Not wanting to pretend that things were other than they were. "Y'all don't know how to do that," she said, her voice much smaller than she intended.

"Do what?"

"Give me what I need."

They rode the rest of the way in silence. She wiped her eyes, rolled down the window, and stuck her head out—riding the rest of the way home with the wind hitting her face.

Carlene's temples throbbed. She could hear the older siblings in the living room. Boyd went in to join them. Nat, Charlie, and Kurt sat around the ancient wooden kitchen table that was scarred and marred with scratches, pencil marks, nail polish stains and such. The kids were making a dinner of cereal and milk in spite of all the food mourners had left.

"Hi Carl."

"Hey." Carlene sat and laid her head on her arms. "How long you staying?" she asked Nat and Charlie.

"Granny's picking us up when she gets off work. She's coming to get our stuff," Charlie explained.

"Where's Baby Carla?" Natalie asked.

"Matthew's."

The kids went back to eating. She watched them sideways. She always missed them. She, Kurt, Charlie, and Natalie had always been a busy quadrangle—figuring things out, putting dinner together, arguing over who ate what, watching television, and now passing Baby Carla around. Carlene bossed them around just the way Eva had done when Sophia left. And Lisa after her. It was a Sawyer legacy. Now the legacy was over. Sophia's daughters had no more of her kids to mother.

Nat and Charlie had been pulled away from the Sawyers and taken back to their mother's side. While Carlene and Kurt's mother had vanished, Natalie and Charlie's mom was as good as gone. That made them all even. Most of the time their mother, Portia, was locked up. When she wasn't locked up, she had a few good days or weeks before she was back picking bugs or scabs or whatever it was itching her so. Or she'd start screaming like she was her very own megaphone, and back to the facility she'd go. Hunt forbade her to come to the house. The last time she got through the front door, he'd said in his deep, but quiet voice, "Don't come here scaring my kids."

"These are my children too. Them two, right there, those are mine." She'd stepped in their direction.

"Woman, I will have you locked so far down in a hole, you'll see the devil's face. Go get in the truck." And he had driven Portia back to her mother's house. But some weekends, when Nat and Charlie went for their visit, their grandma brought them back at some random hour; nobody had to mention that Portia was over there raving like a mad woman.

Carlene raised her head, her eyes traveling from Nat, to Charlie, to Kurt. "You can come back when you need to."

Charlie whispered back. "We can't. Y'all are going with Aunt Edna and Uncle Gabe. Granny says the house is probably gonna be sold."

"I'm not leaving," Carlene responded. With her head still laying on her arms, she reached out and touched Natalie. "You guys can come anytime you want. I'll watch you." The tears were back, and they would not stop flowing as she cried for all she was losing. She'd already lost enough. No one moved, nor did they speak. The trio would not leave until Carlene released them. Finally, she pulled her mind onto the next five minutes. Willed herself to think about soap and warm water. She turned away from the scraping raw feeling inside that could easily kill her, or at least send her screaming to the asylum like Portia. Carlene wiped her face on her sleeve and sniffled. She rose to take a shower—her first in she didn't remember how many days. "Clean the table before you leave the kitchen," she said over her shoulder. Just before she went into the bedroom, she turned and went back to the table. "Again with the tears," she said, forcing a smile. She opened her arms to the young ones so they would come to her. They clung to each other for a very long time.

Carlene emerged from the bathroom in a brown plaid robe that had been around as long as any of them could remember. Her hands were filled with tufts of hair she'd just cut off. Ever since she became a mother, Carlene began cutting it herself when she got out of the shower—lifting it section by section and snipping it off with the heavy shears her mother had used to cut fabric. She kept it cut down to a ragged inch all over her head—ragged because the scissors were dull, and none of them knew about sharpening. She would squeeze the clippings dry in a wad of tissue, then burn them. When their mother finished combing hair, she had always pulled the tufts from the comb and brush and done the same. Hair was very powerful, Sophia claimed, and you never wanted it to fall into anybody else's hands. That was one of the clearest memories Carlene had of her mother.

Carlene stepped on the back porch carrying an ashtray filled with hair and a book of matches. Eva sat holding her youngest in one of the old kitchen chairs against the house. The legs were splayed, and dirty cotton tufts sprouted from cracked plastic. The sun was setting, but the evening was warm.

"God almighty, the funeral was awful. Aunt Edna collapsed. Fell out so completely coma-like that they had to call the rescue squad. The funeral just about stopped. They thought she was dead for a minute."

"Wow."

"I know. It was awful. It was one of the most awful days I have ever lived."

"Thank God I didn't go. These days are already awful enough."

Eva continued. "We were waiting for you to get back. We were scared when you didn't come home."

"Boyd told me."

"Kurt said, 'She'll be back. Trust me.'"

Now that the funeral was over, and Eva didn't have a point to make, Carlene relaxed in her sister's company. A stray cat walked across the yard and rubbed against the clothesline pole. Then it strolled beneath the shelter to get lost in a fray of broken furniture, old toys, and dead appliances. Soon Hunt would have had some guys help him load it on his truck and carry it to the junkyard. Memories and thoughts swirled like wash water. "You think Momma can feel that her husband died? I mean, now that you're married, if something happened to Dan, do you think you would feel it?"

At once Carlene wanted to snatch back the words. Eva's features immediately narrowed into her mama-by-default grimace and her voice crept down a notch. "Sophia Sawyer probably wouldn't feel it if we all burned up in this rat hole right this minute."

A chill ran through Carlene. "That's mean. You don't know that. You always say crap you don't know shit about."

"Oh please. Think about it. So much has already happened to us. Cook ran away. I almost died when I had Fallon—remember, I almost bled to death. She knows where we live. One of three things is going on with Sophia: 1) That sixth sense you're talking about isn't working, and she has no instincts at all. 2) If it is working, she has no conscience, or 3) She's dead."

"You've given this some thought."

"Too much thought to suit me." Eva lit a cigarette from the cigarette and shifted her baby to the other knee. "Don't waste your time wondering about Sophia, okay?" She looked over at Carlene. "You have more important things to think about."

"Okay." Carlene thought of her older sisters who had both had their turn as mothers of the house. Way before the time they should have been trusted with anybody's kids. They were bad mothers. Not the kind a person would want at all. They cussed and shoved and bossed, and they didn't care if they made you cry. The house was always too hot or too cold. Maybe they didn't know to open curtains to let in the sun, or open windows to let breezes flow through. And they were horrid cooks—so horrid that Carlene made a habit of frying as much bacon as she could get her hands on—just to taste the salty, crunchy, delicious strips. And she saved the pan grease in a jar to pour over their bland rubbery meats and mushy starches. The pounds had piled on month by month until Carlene was a 5'3" orb.

Yes, her sisters had been the ones who bandaged up the bruises, stuck lunch money in their backpacks, put Kotex under the bathroom sink, did endless loads of laundry, and said yes or no to second helpings—but blame blared loud with every action. It seemed the younger ones were punished for stealing the teenaged lives they craved. Because the sisters worked like wicked stepmothers from fairytales. But even so, they could never get a handle on their charges. They couldn't stop Kurt from wetting the bed, couldn't stop Lisa from fucking a different boy every month in her junior high school stairwell. Nor could they stop Cook from packing up and leaving and going God knows where—never so much as calling any one of them ever again.

Carlene looked over at Eva—who pulled on the cigarette so hard her jaws caved in. For the first time, Carlene realized that Eva's salty nature wasn't her fault. And Carlene had learned from these sister how not to be. Because she never made Kurt, Nat or Charlie cry, and whatever she got, she shared with them. And Carlene knew she was sweet to Baby Carla. She held out her index and middle fingers to take a drag of Eva's cigarette. Eva handed it over. "Thanks Eva," she said to her sister.

Edna called ahead to make sure Carlene would be home. They had to finalize the move is what she'd said. "Let's go to Kilpatricks so we can talk." Carlene was ready for her aunt when she pulled up in her red Honda Civic hatchback. It was Tuesday. Boyd was already gone. Eva was still hanging around; Dan would pick them all up on Friday when he got off work. Lisa would ride with them.

Aunt Edna and Carlene rode to the grill that was greasy but maintained. A place anybody in Haden didn't mind having a bite. Two of the women who had worked with Sophia were still servers, and they always gave Carlene something extra for free.

"So how's the baby?" Aunt Edna asked.

"She's with her daddy for a few days. She's fine."

"Good. It's going to be fun having her around. You got your stuff together?"

Carlene shook her head.

"Kurt says he'll be ready tomorrow. I think he wants to get out before everybody leaves. He'll be too sad if he's the last to leave. I know this is so hard for you all."

One of Sophia's old coworkers came to the table. She touched them both on the shoulders, asked how they were doing, said she'd keep them in her prayers. "Order what you want. On the house. It's the least I can do."

They thanked her, and just ordered coffee—a whole pot. Carlene picked at her fingernails and looked at them under the table, gathering courage. "Aunt Edna, I'm not going to live with you."

"Carlene, don't. Honey, no. I can't even…" Edna shook her head, stopped speaking, closed her eyes. She took some deep breaths and continued. "The day Hunt died, I pulled you to the side, and I told you he had sat at my table two weeks to the day before he died and asked me to take care of you and Carla and Kurt. It's clear to me now he knew he was going. And I promised him."

"I know."

"I think we need to respect what he wanted. What he specifically asked for. You love your daddy. Don't you think for the next couple of years, you can go along with his wishes?"

"I think Daddy was just thinking about my age. But Aunt Edna, I'll just stay at the house and live in it. Just like I've been doing."

"Oh no. That's crazy," Edna said. "You cannot stay there by yourself. I think that's illegal even. You're a child."

"I'm not a child, and it's not illegal. I'm old enough to get married. I'm old enough to make decisions. I have a baby." Carlene took a sip of the bitter black coffee. It was what was called for. "Ask Gabriel when a girl becomes a woman in Guatemala."

"Well, I know that. It's 15."

"Exactly, with the quincenera and everything. Just because I'm 16 doesn't mean I'm not ready to be grown. Daddy was just being a father when he asked you. He had to ask for Kurt. Kurt's only 12. But I've been running the house since Lisa left. Since I was 13. Daddy's in and out and stays where he wants to, when he feels like it. He never came home every night, you know?"

"But still. He was there more often than not."

"But Aunt Edna, I've been telling myself what to do."

Aunt Edna's coffee was cooling, and her eyes were red and swelling with tears that she dabbed carefully from the corners. "Think about Carla. She needs steady, stable mothering. She can't ride all over the county on the back of your bike whenever you get the notion. She's a baby."

"I know that. Probably nobody knows this, but Aunt Edna, I'm really smart."

"Really? How are you so smart, Carlene?" There was a light moment, and Aunt Edna smiled.

"I have made the honor roll every semester I've been in high school. And I don't even go to school everyday. While having a baby."

"That's an accomplishment. I'm glad. I'm proud of you."

"Thank you. And Aunt Edna, nobody has made me do that. I have been my own mother for a really long time now. So it wasn't fair for Daddy to lump me in with Kurt and Nat and Charlie like I'm some clueless kid. I've had my freedom and been running the house for three years. I'm the one that makes Kurt and Nat and Charlie do what they do. And I know everybody thinks I'm wild. And maybe I am. But they eat everyday, and Daddy's not cooking and calling the shots. He doesn't wake us up in the morning. He doesn't say when to wash the clothes."

"I get the picture. These are good examples of why you feel like you do. But you're still young."

"Aunt Edna, I'd make your life a living hell." It was written all over the older woman's face that she had nothing to offer a girl like Carlene. Aunt Edna was soft and had her easy life with her husband. It took her a whole afternoon to bake a chicken and make a pot of stew. Aunt Edna made special trips to get her special foods, and everything was like an event. It would be enough for her to keep up with what Kurt needed. It wouldn't be fair to load her down with a whole family and expect her to rise to the occasion. Carlene knew she could do more in a day with one hand tied behind her back than Aunt Edna could in two or three days.

"Well that would be a choice, Carlene. You decide how you're going to treat somebody. And that wouldn't be right to come in telling me how you'll mess up my life."

"I don't mean it like that. I'm just saying. If I can't stay home, I rather go to some temporary living situation or something. After all this time, I can't pretend I need a mother to take care of me."

"I'm not trying to be your mother."

"Aunt Edna, that's what women do. As soon as Eva and Lisa come home, they try to start telling me what to do, what to think. It's not like me and you would be roommates. The most I could stand is a roommate." Carlene refilled her own cup with coffee. It was going down easy, and she thought of her father—the way he drank his coffee and smoked a cigarette like they were the two best things in his day. She reached into the pocket of her hooded sweatshirt and took out a Salem. She lit it, and blew the smoke from the corner of her mouth, away from Aunt Edna. "I got a few habits I can stand to lose, but I'm not scared to do what I have to do."

"You say this like it's a fact. I'm not there with you Carlene. I'm seeing this from a whole different perspective. I promised my brother."

"Like Daddy never broke a promise. I love you Aunt Edna, so why can't you just check on me? Baby-sit for me now and then. I'll be 17 in a couple of months. I figured out already I'll get a part-time job so I can pay the house insurance and taxes."

"What do you know about house insurance and taxes?"

"I write the checks. I know how much the bills are. I know when they're due. I can do the math. Just help me. Let me put you on the daycare paper as my emergency contact. That way if I get off late or something, you can pick Baby Carla up. Stuff like that. That's what I need. I don't need to pack up and leave a house I'm already in charge of."

Aunt Edna took in a breath. "I don't know."

"You know. When Momma left, she turned us into women. Daddy had no way of stopping that unless he was going to stay home and watch us everyday and night, and all weekend. I'm already a mother."

"And that is really important Carlene. If somehow you get to live on your own, you have to be the best mother you can be to your daughter. That's a lot for somebody your age."

She looked at her aunt across the table. Edna looked down into the coffee cup. "I'll do my best, Aunt Edna. And Matthew is a decent father, and his family loves her. So they'll help out. But Aunt Edna, really, Baby Carla's going to be fine."

"Maybe we can try it your way for a while. But I will check on you everyday. Because I'm not comfortable Carlene."

"That's fair. And let Kurt spend the night sometimes." Staring across the table, Carlene wondered if Aunt Edna would really check on her the way she said she would. Would she baby-sit and bring a meal? Aunt Edna seemed limp. Like losing her brother had deflated her. Eva said Aunt Edna had actually passed out at the funeral. *I'd be crazy to go live with you*, Carlene said to herself and closed her case. She relaxed a little—enough to order a burger. She had not eaten much in the past few days. She coaxed Aunt Edna to order something too, especially since it was on the house. When the order came, Carlene took large bites—finding her hunger once the decision was made.

By Sunday afternoon, the house was empty, and the coming and going was over. That night Carlene had swept Hunt's dresser top items into a grocery bag and stuffed it in the bottom of his closet: Mennen deodorant, store brand lotion, a tin can of change, a pocket knife, a pocket flashlight, his wallet, a bottle opener, and paper—bank statements, check stubs, ripped slivers with numbers scrawled on them. Carlene changed the sheets on Hunt's bed, and claimed it as her own. She added Mrs. Rowson's throw to the bed because she and Baby Carla needed the comfort of soft and warm. And if she and Baby Carla slept in the big bed together, maybe they wouldn't be so lonely. And maybe Hunt's angel spirit would hover around them.

The alarm clock beeped at 6:30 Monday morning. Carlene was bone tired. She'd had a fretful first night of awakening to a racing heart and unquenchable thirst, of creeping through the house to drink water, and sleeping with the lights on. She was glad she had called the daycare teacher Friday night. She said it would be fine to bring Baby Carla in her pajamas. "Take it slow," is what the woman said. "Don't overwhelm yourself." Carlene was listening to any advice anybody had. Not saying she would take it. But she was a woman now, and there was no fall back. She had to be at school everyday. "If you don't," Eva had said, "They will snatch you and Baby Carla up so fast you won't know your ass from your elbow."

So at 6:55, Carlene took the keys off the hook, grabbed her backpack, and ran outdoors to warm up the truck. She ran back for Baby Carla and carefully strapped her in. First stop day care. School by 7:30. One day at a time.

# EVA - 1997

Eva Peroe and her girls had been in town just long enough for some to pity the children the absence of a daddy. Long enough for a few to speculate about whether the long, lean woman with glued-on jeans had ever even had a husband. And definitely long enough for others to begrudge Eva for the three or four men that seemed always to be coming and going from her house. A handful of Paxton residents, a minority for sure, wanted to know the truth about her and her children, who, in the past ten months, seemed so different from everybody else in town. They looked different from other Paxtoners—all of them thin as wire with hair that often went several days without any obvious contact with a comb. The Peroes kept no regular habits—up late nights, sleeping days, walking down the aisles of Zip Mart at midnight.

The only truth worth knowing was that Eva had married young, and she did have a husband three counties over. She had married Dan Peroe a few weeks after her eighteenth birthday. They had five children before she caught her breath. Then, suddenly she was not pregnant or falling desperately in love with a brand new baby; and her husband was driving long distance trucks. "Ain't no other way I can find to make enough money to feed all these people," he'd said.

"They're not people. They're little children. How much do they eat? You can find something closer than all over the country."

"Where?" he challenged. "And what they don't eat, they make up for in Pampers. Tell me they don't."

So Dan was gone for five, seven, sometimes ten or fifteen days at a time. All Eva could think about was whores. Whores waiting at rest stops, behind the stall doors just dying to suck him off for a very affordable $5. Alone in her bed night after night, Eva would close her eyes and see tiny, pink panties attached to Dan's fingers creeping over young, round butt cheeks. Long smooth legs climbed up into the cab of his eighteen-wheeler and he leaned into the strangers' arms. Sometimes she imagined him bringing home a converted whore and asking for a divorce. And on and on. These brief waking nightmares played over and over like stuck 45 records.

When Dan made it home, he'd collapse into the bed and sleep for inhuman lengths of time. Nobody but a man who'd been screwing like a rabbit could sleep for fifteen hours straight, Eva thought. While he slept, Eva changed clothes three or four times a day—first into something tight and sexy, but then, catching her silhouette in a mirror, she'd cover her flimsy belly in a loose tee shirt. Then she'd see a commercial featuring some cock tease, and she'd try another tight something to show off her blooming mommy breasts. By the time she and Dan were both awake and in the same room, Eva was livid. Livid. "Why the hell can't you get a job like everybody else? You just want to whore all over the friggin country is why."

"You're a damn lunatic is what the hell you are. I bring home twice the money I did before. And what is all this nonsense about whoring? I'm not trying to pick up some cock-rotting disease. I'm not stupid. You're crazy."

But Eva was not convinced. She took to smelling his laundry and examining it with the precision of a spy. She did all this while he slept, before she washed his clothes. Or she'd turn over in bed and thoughts assailed her like rabid dogs, and she'd creep out of bed and pore over his wallet—one slip of paper at a time. They were maddening activities, and she could never find anything conclusive. And sometimes what looked like something couldn't be quite nailed down into anything specific. And God forbid if one of the children came in while she was sniffing something. It was not a good place to be.

On a particular night, Eva worked up a fever trying to have a conversation with her husband. Four dropped calls and seven *The party you have reached is unavailable* kept her up all night long. While she dialed and dialed and dialed and dialed and dialed, another part of her brain fished for a rational intervention. But something quivering and afraid was growing monstrously stronger, and Eva was stuck in a loop—unable to get Dan and his whereabouts off her mind. Unable to even lay the phone down on the table and tend to the crying baby.

In an instant, Eva wondered if this feeling—this humiliating hunger for the raw truth, was what had driven her mother away from their home. If the not-knowing could snatch a mind and keep it out of reach. Eva put down the receiver and surrendered. As soon as day broke, she packed the kids into their roomy, well-worn Plymouth Acclaim and drove an hour and a half. "We need a break," she told her children.

"A break from what?" Fallon asked.

"I need a little break from your daddy."

"Daddy's never home anyway," Fallon said.

"Well, a break from too much stress, " she replied, and looking sideways at the girl, and in the rearview mirror at the others, she could see the questions forming on their foreheads. "Stress is something you can't understand yet. Stress is not for kids. Stress is what makes me smoke all these cigarettes."

Eva found a cheap, drafty three-bedroom house with a sprawling dirt yard out in the country. Immediately Eva felt much better. It was like she'd found a new kind of air. There was nothing around her but dirt and trees. There was no waiting for Dan's phone calls or reviewing her stretch marks. There was no underwear to sniff. Just her and her kids.

    They fell into a loose rhythm of living. They ate when and what they wanted. Sometimes they'd eat bologna sandwiches all day long and drink Pepsi. Or they might just buy and eat an entire box of cereal and milk. Hotdogs were popular, and so were Sloppy Joes. Eva and the children slept long and hard from spending most of their time outdoors. And often the house didn't wake up till long after the school bus was gone. With the distance from Dan, and all the kids sleeping through the night, Eva was finally able to fathom that it was possible to sleep like the dead for an inhuman number of hours.

Although Eva lived in the house in the middle of nowhere, men discovered her. They discovered her in the Zip Mart, at the gas station, and one found her walking down the side of the road carrying a gas can to fill her car. Eva figured it was the happiness in her that magnetized them, because it was the first time in her life that she felt happy at least most of the time.

    "I can't beat them off. And I don't even have to give 'em none," she told her younger sister, Lisa.

    "Well, that is a miracle. You must have some kind of magic spell put on you. The opposite of mine. I have yet to meet the man without magic panty-removing powers."

Duke Sutter, the first man Eva met, was pretty much a Friday night man. He showed up near dusk with a bottle of wine or liquor, and sat at the dining room table talking a lot. He wore laced, leather shoes and a sport hat—no matter the weather. He was older—fortyish. Eva liked him because he had a soft voice that would've put her to sleep easily if they'd been in bed in the dark, but she never went to bed with Duke, and he never spent the night. He just sat and talked and talked and drank and drank until his color changed and his eyes became slivered almonds. He'd talk on about the government, and how it didn't matter one way or another who was in office because they were puppets of the world billionaires. He talked about being fooled by the news, and how smart she was to stay away from people and all their opinions that would poison her mind and make her into something she wasn't. Eva felt smart and wise when he talked about her. Then he would say, "Alright Eva. I'll see you around." Eva would hug his neck and thank him for coming to see her, then watch him back around in her yard and glide slowly up the road in his Buick.

"What about Daddy?" Jillene asked Eva when Duke Sutter began showing up from time to time.

"Daddy's got his own life, and he's plenty busy."

"Does Daddy know this man? Is he Daddy's friend too?"

"This man isn't Daddy's business. Just like what Daddy's doing right this very minute is none of my business." Eva set her mouth, and clinched her teeth, and lit a cigarette. Like dust from a sudden wind, her own father blew across her mind. How he was out fathering children with only God knew who while her mother tended to the children.

The other man was Stanley Davis. He came different days during the week—depending on his shift. He was large and loud, and he drove a dump truck and wore a hard hat, and he looked somewhat like an action figure. He fit right in with the Peroes, because he liked being outdoors as much as they did. He would pull up in the truck, get out, and stand in the middle of the yard, asking or answering questions. Then he might sit in a yard chair and look around at the trees, up in the sky, and sometimes nod off. From time to time, he'd wheel the kids' banana seat bike unsteadily around the yard with the children chasing him like he was entertainment. After a while Eva would come out, or he would go in. But they never seemed to be in a hurry because he did spend the night. He always took a tub bath, drank a good deal of Hi-C, and went to bed when Eva did. When he stayed, Eva usually got up early and got the children out to school on time. Then Eva and Stanley would go in town and eat country ham and eggs with biscuits.

This was all working for Eva. With a life of her own, she could actually love Dan without having to trust him. Eva believed it was the trusting that always got the best of a wife. But a call from Dan when he was 100 miles out of town, asking if she'd be home, didn't involve any trust at all. It involved only a choice. So when Dan had a particularly good load, he would stop by and drop off the envelopes filled with money that still paid the rent and bought the food. Five or six hundred dollars, sometimes a thousand or two at a time. Eva would stand in the doorway watching the kids enjoy him. Eventually she warmed up to the idea of treating him like the husband that he still was. Because he was still her husband. They didn't have a legal divorce, or even a separation. He always spent the night—careful to "cover it up" (as he called it), because he and Eva together seemed so full of fertilizer. For that day or two, Eva could breathe and laugh and take Dan at face value. She wasn't looking for the lie beneath his eyes, or the words between the lines. The next day he would be gone, and she didn't think about where he was going, when he would be back, and who he'd meet along the way.

But with all this living going on, the kids missed a lot of school.

"Ms. Noon said I need to come to school everyday. And if I'm sick, I need to bring a note. But she said I need to be very sick to stay out. Sick enough to go to the doctor," Fallon told Eva.

"The principal gave me this paper," Jillene said when she brought home a letter with Attendance Officer printed in bold at the top.

Pete's kindergarten progress card had his number of absences written in red with a sad face stamped beside it.

And there were official letters, and intermittent phone calls from a robot-like voice. But Eva somehow let it all pass. They were her children, and they were happy. If everybody was happy, that seemed like some kind of magical feat in and of itself. There was plenty of time to work up to regularity.

But one day, a car drove up. Two women got out of the car. Eva later figured they came in pairs because they were liable to get hurt sooner or later, with the kind of business they were in. They proceeded to knock, and Eva let them in.

"We've come from the county office for public schools," the light-haired woman said. "The school district is concerned about the welfare of your children."

Eva invited them to sit down, and she sat with them and listened carefully. They had very much to say about attendance. Apparently Eva hadn't responded the way they wanted, so they had a computer paper printed out of all the times they'd tried to contact her. Eva remembered seeing one of the women—the dark-haired one, in Food Fare.

Once they'd stated all their facts, Eva responded with, "Yes, I received some calls to go to school."

"Well why didn't you come?"

*Because sometimes we stay up late, and sometimes the clock doesn't go off, and sometimes we have company, and sometimes, sometimes, things don't happen at all like you plan*, Eva thought.

But she said, "I must have meant to. It must have slipped my mind."

The light-haired one explained in slow, carefully-chosen words that all three children were at risk of being held over in their grades for failing to attend school regularly. This warranted social welfare involvement. "It is your job to send them to school, and you're not doing it."

"I'll send them," Eva said meekly.

"You'll have to. Our office has been called to help monitor their attendance and make home visits to make sure things are going alright. We advocate for the children. For their education. Do you understand what we're saying to you, Mrs. Peroe?"

"Yes."

"We're not here for you to say what we want to hear. We're here to make sure you know that it's the law for children to be sent to school every day, as long as they're healthy. And when they're not healthy, it's the law that they get a teacher to come to the home." She kept saying law in a harsh tone. "Education is that important, Mrs. Peroe. It's a legal matter, so we have to monitor your children," the dark-haired woman said in a slicing voice.

"There's no reason for all that," Eva said. "I can get them to school." She fished a warm, limp cigarette from her crumbled soft pack of Benson and Hedges and lit it. Eva thought back to her own school days. Nobody had ever come to their home and pressured their father to send them to school everyday. Sometimes school wasn't on the front burner. Just like the year their mother left. They mostly did what they felt like doing—and most times, they didn't feel like doing much. It was a year of cold rooms and crying. Even at 27, Eva could almost taste the raw, deep fear of those months. She had been afraid for three whole seasons, and would not sleep alone. Could not sleep without the touch of a sister's arm or foot or hand near by. After a while she had managed to organize them into a tight knot of activity that got them back close to normal. All the while she tried to make her mother proud of her by being the woman Sophia had asked her to be. But Sophia had no way of knowing what Eva did, and their lives never became normal enough to make them want to stay. Their home became a place to leave as soon as there was a reason to go.

The woman was still talking on and on. "And we always want to work with the mothers to help them do right by their children, so if you have any questions, or if you need help with something, you call either one of us. We will leave our cards. The worst thing that can happen is you need help with something, don't get it, and something goes wrong. Because when things go wrong, we have a protocol to follow."

"Do you understand?" the light-haired social worker backed her up.

Eva nodded. A sadness so grave ran through her body that she had to stand up and leave the room. "I'll be right back." Eva went into the kitchen and stood against the sink. The sound of her children playing rode the wind through the window. Aside for the children, she always felt alone. Between their words, these women were hiding little threats about separating mothers from children. Eva could feel it.

The visit left Eva with resentment so strong that she wanted nothing more than to get them. She didn't know how exactly, but an anger in her belly lasted through the night and kept her restless, disturbed, and awake till the witching hour. When she finally dropped off, her sleep was filled with untanglings and near falls, missed heartbeats, and sweat. Voices pierced her dreams, with people speaking words that didn't rightfully belong to them. Dan issued subtle threats about taking the wrong birth control pills. The school social worker ridiculed her for being unable to satisfy a simple man. Her childhood friend chastised her for feeding her youngest son garbage. Her mother, Sophia, was waving goodbye from a landlocked ocean liner.

Eva awakened that morning before dawn—edgy and annoyed from just two hours of sleep. Nobody could tell her what to do. Nobody could come into her life, dangle fear in front of her, and expect her to wait around for some bitch of a surprise.

Of all the things that had happened in her life, Eva had never worried about her children. They seemed attached to her like her limbs. Nobody really thought about their knees or their necks, unless something had gone seriously wrong with them. People always told her, "You have a lot of children to be so young." They said it all the time. "That's not a problem," Eva always responded. She never worried about them falling, or dropping things, or losing their belongings. She didn't worry about them passing their grades, or catching cold. She didn't worry about whether they gained or lost weight or friends. The last thing she ever wanted to worry about were her children—the only real proof she'd ever had that love actually existed.

That morning, Eva sat on the back steps with a cigarette and a cup of instant coffee. She surveyed her surroundings: muddy toys strewn here and there, scrawny bushes struggling from lack of attention, the peeling edges of the painted porch, the aluminum siding swinging loose on the rented house. She clutched the coffee mug close to her chin—let the steam mix with the smoke and warm her face. In her mind, she was already packing their clothes and loading the car. There was no need to say good-bye to anybody at all. It was just a town, and it was not her home. She would catch up with Dan when she got where she was going. She could already hear Fallon asking, "What are we moving for? Stress?"

"Yes," she would answer. "Sometimes things go wrong, and life just makes you leave."

# COOK AND MARINA — 2004

From the moment Cook left for his latest trek to the city, Marina has thought only of her own departure. While her father, Cook, takes short trips away from their home to scavenge for what they need, and to hustle up enough money to buy what he can't scavenge, Marina knows that when she leaves, she's leaving for good. Her body is crawling with expectation. She is four months past her thirteenth birthday, and everyday since then has built a case for her moving on. For the past two days, she's kept one eye out for Cook's return. When she finally sees her father approaching, or rather, when she hears his footsteps crunching in the forest, Marina prepares herself.

Cook walks into the yard and places the sack on the bench. Before he can divulge the contents, Marina runs up. "Hi Daddy." Marina glances briefly in the bag — only canned goods, rice and other grains, toilet paper, old magazines and newspapers, some clothing. Lots of stick matches. Cookies, sweetened drinks, or other treats rarely appear. Slow poison, Cook calls them; although Marina is sure she sometimes hears and smells the so-called lethal confections gnashed between Cook and Rose's teeth after their children are in bed.

"Missed you, baby," he says leaning towards her. The bottom of his face is a tangle of black prickly hairs. She dodges the kiss that will scratch if it meets her cheek.

Cook shouts to the rest of the family: his wife, Rose, and his sons, Jacob and Boyd. "I'm back!"

Marina says, "I have to talk to you and Mama. It's important."

"Okay. Talk to me."

"I said you and Mama."

Cook looks at her. Raises his brow. "Rosie! Rose! Come out here!" he yells for his wife. Rose comes to the trailer door and steps carefully down the uneven cinder blocks. She touches Cook's arm; he moves towards his wife till they are side-by-side with no space between them.

Marina tells them, "I'm going into the city. I'm leaving here."

"Going to the city? To do what?" Cook draws in his chin to emphasize his confusion.

"To live. I'm not staying out here for the rest of my life."

"The rest of your life? You're a friggin kid. Do you know what'll happen to you if you go wandering in the city?"

"I'll turn myself into the authorities," Marina says. She says this softly. She knows Cook hears disease, plague, and unmentionable evil when the word authorities is mentioned. Rose stands silently, her face a chiseled work of art softened only by darting, doe-shaped eyes.

"The authorities can't help you. In their machines, you weren't even born!"

Rose lowers her head. She is ashamed to have borne her children beyond the walls of doctors and hospitals—with no certificates acknowledging their births. Cook is proud that he has brought his own children into the world—cutting the cords and being the first to touch their shriveled bodies.

Marina walks to the back of the trailer, and yells louder, "They have bureaus and welfare for children!"

"THEY HAVE BUREAUS AND WELFARE FOR CHILDREN!" Cook mocks her, his voice echoing like the wrath of God. Just hearing her mention these words brings memories of the shelters and hostels in which he spent his 16th through 18th years. Dozens of nights, with candles flickering within the trailer, Cook has terrorized his children with stories of rape and brutality, of food too rancid for dogs, of paid caretakers who should rot beneath the darkest prisons.

"Why didn't you go back home?" Marina always asks Cook. "You had a family."

"New York is a long way from Haden. And when you leave home the way I did, you never think about returning." When Cook was 15, he had crept into his father's room as he slept. As sneaky as fog, he had slipped all the money from Hunt's wallet and from the back of the drawer—beneath his undershirts. The next day, Cook was on the bus, heading for New York City—a dazzling oasis 450 miles away. For months, terror clung like vines around Cook's heart as he managed to survive in alleys and behind dumpsters, and sometimes in the clutches of men who deserved castration. For years now, these memories have turned Cook's stomach.

Marina's anger is so hot that it's drying her tears before they surface. She sits at the back steps of the trailer. She hears her brothers playing mouse-like inside. Both boys are quiet and have the same obscure ways, even though they are two years apart.

Rose scurries around inside the trailer, then thunders down the steps past Marina. Rose carries Marina's crate of reading materials across the yard and down the slope to the creek. She hurls the contents into the water and steps in—stomping trance-like on the magazines and books ranging from *The Selected Writings of Emerson* to *Beloved*, to *Zen and the Art of Motorcycle Maintenance* to *How to Eat to Live*. There are scores of *Marvel* comic books and popular magazines.

Rose rips pages, roughs her feet over the piles, destroys as much as she can before it floats up stream. "All this shit in her head!" Rose screams, her eyes casting bullets of fear and pain in Marina's direction.

Cook props his foot on the step next to Marina. "Believe it or not, I'm giving you the best chance you'll ever have. In this lifetime, you were born my daughter. This is your best chance. Right here. Believe it or not. Be thankful."

Marina cannot find her voice. She knows that if she opens her mouth, she will scream and bite and kick and scratch. His words have become poison to her. Whenever Cook speaks these days, something ugly swells up inside her and she feels it must be death. If she stays here, this rising death will take her over—no matter what he says. Marina rolls her eyes, turns from Cook, and walks in the opposite direction. Their hope is not hers. Hope for her is away from here. Hope for them is only here.

Marina's earliest memory is of lying in the back of a van half asleep, listening to songs peal out of the radio. The memories are faint now—like comics that have endured countless downpours. In those days, the boys weren't born. Cook, Rose, and Marina went places all the time. Onto highways, to the zoo, into stores and gas stations. Songs accompanied them wherever they went. Words would play in her head over and over. She dreams some of the songs. In her dreams she hears words to a melody, mere slivers of songs. A line plays over and over in her dreams. Sometimes Marina sits and tries to remember more—and she feels a frustration rising, knowing songs and melodies exist, and she is cut off from it all.

Then one day, shortly after Jacob was born, there was a problem with the van. It couldn't be moved, and a truck towed it to a pound. At Cook's insistence, Rose went from building to building, office to office, desk to desk—asking, pleading, and debating with people to return the van or waive the fees. Cook was out trying to scrape together an impossible sum to get the van released and repaired. Finally, at the end of the day, Rose sat on a bench and sobbed with Jacob hanging loosely from her arms. "Please somebody just give us back our van. It's our home! My husband has nothing. Help us, Jesus. Please just help us. See my babies, I have two babies here." Nobody helped.

At sunset, they met Cook in Fort Greene Park. Cook had bundled up all their belongings from the van, and had them slung across his back. Cook paced and expounded late into the night about blood-sucking vultures, trifling whores, and the myths of God. He swore and beat the air with his fists, saying strange words that rendered them all silent.

"Let's try to get to your father. He'll take us in. Get money for the bus. Please," Rose finally said when he took a breath.

"Never. I took all he had. I have to be man enough to make my own way. I'm a man."

That same night, when there was no hope of reclaiming the van, Cook waited in the shadows of the Nevins Street subway station until, nearing three a.m., a gentle man with a loose tie emerged. "I just need your money. Just keep your mouth shut. Don't say one word that might get you hurt," Cook had whispered through clinched teeth. The man, who smelled of sweet wine, did as he was told. Cook searched the man, took his cell phone, and snapped it. Cook walked slightly behind him, escorted him down DeKalb Avenue, and sent the jittery victim into the park. "Don't turn around cause we're watching you. Keep walking north till you come out the Myrtle side," Cook hissed.

As soon as the man was out of his sight, Cook broke into and hotwired a gray Honda Accord—a car so ordinary it would be impossible to pick out. He picked up his family and headed north—over the bridge, up the FDR, over the George Washington Bridge, up the Palisades, and out of the city. It was daybreak when he parked off a back road and left them at the edge of a wooded area. For several days, Rose, Marina, and Jacob stayed close to the car awaiting Cook's return. Finally hunger and filth drove Rose out of the car and onto the street. She left five-year-old Marina to care for her putrid, screaming baby brother.

By nightfall, Rose was back at the car with bologna, peanut butter, bread, juice, and cheap towels to be used for diapers.

Days passed before Cook returned. Days that lingered like gauzy webs. Rose left them four or five more times before Cook finally knocked on the car's window in the middle of the night. Marina was ecstatic.

Cook had slept all day. In the middle of the next night, Cook drove several miles, then deserted the stolen car on a residential street. He walked his family west, miles deep into the upstate woods. They followed Cook down a complex trail marked by bottles, papers, rags, and sticks. At last they came to a weathered trailer that stood several yards away from a narrow creek. Rose entered slowly, her palms pressed against her cheeks. She touched a rusting rod and reel propped against a dirt-colored couch heaped with pillows and blankets. She touched the end tables and lamps, moved across the room to a kitchen table and chairs, then finally stood at a sink filled with beer cans and unwashed dishes, pots, and pans. Above the sink hung a 1987 calendar frozen on the month of August.

Cook had touched the calendar. "Seeing as how they've been gone nine years, I don't think they're coming back."

"This is a miracle. Thank you God," Rose said.

"No. Thank you, Cook Sawyer." Cook's face had broken into a rare smile as he touched his wife's face. "You cannot imagine how long it took me to find this place. I knew there had to be something somewhere. All these cabins and fishing spots. It was only a matter of time.

Marina walks to the edge of the creek to examine the remnants of her library. Rose's outburst provides further evidence that it is time to go. Marina's mind is filled with pictures of girls, boys, men, and women whose faces glow beneath electric lights. She imagines wearing beautiful clothes that fit her body, riding in cars, and eating dinners in restaurants with so many friends that she can't remember all their names.

It baffles Marina that Rose and Cook want so little. "Did you ever have these things?" she has asked Rose, pointing to pictures in magazines.

"No," is Rose's usual response.

"Did you see them?" Marina has asked.

"All the time."

"Did you want them?"

"Yeah."

Cook has different answers. He has had some. He has seen plenty. Marina knows that Rose and Cook have something between them that makes this isolation bearable. Cook is all Rose has ever had. They found each other on trips to Coney Island, rides on the ferry, and excursions led by Mt. Secretto's Youth Hostel counselors. Both Rose and Cook were loners; they gravitated toward each other when seatmates and partners were required. Her life was his, and vice versa. They have words and memories that came before this place that bind them to each other. Nothing flows from them to bind Marina, however. Blood is not thick enough to destroy her dreams.

When everyone is sleeping, Marina creeps out of the trailer and fills one of Cook's bags with raw potatoes, tomatoes, cucumbers, pole beans, a jar of water, a blanket, and a dress. She walks off into the woods in the direction that Cook always does.

The darkness is familiar, and Marina is not afraid. Her shoes are hard and ill fitting. They rub her heels and toes.

She removes them. The bottom of the forest is carpeted with twigs, moss, pine needles, cones, burrs, stones, and live creatures. The sensation of stepping repeatedly on the unknown causes too much tension for Marina to bear. Her body is tight and her back aches. She replaces her shoes and concentrates on putting a vast distance between herself and the trailer before daybreak.

Her thoughts are strung together in a loose, continuous snarl. Fear of what lies ahead of the forest is punctuated by excitement of what she has seen in the pictures. Rose and Cook's voices weave in and out with a lifetime of warnings and criticisms that Marina feels cannot be true. If nothing beautiful exists in the world, then how would it be possible for people to write about such things? Take pictures of them. Beauty and goodness do exist. Her certainty propels her, and even as fatigue weights her body, Marina continues. At one point she realizes that her face is wet with tears, but her mind is too far away to know why.

The sun rises and sets three times before Marina makes it to the highway. She has only paused to eat, but several times she has awakened unaware that she stopped to sleep. By the time she hears cars traveling the highway, Marina's hair is matted with dirt and leaves, her clothes are damp and muddied, and her feet are bloodied and blistered. She has eaten all but the last raw potato.

Marina walks down the side of the highway along the embankment. It is mid morning when she spots an expanse of grass, some benches, and a short ways off— houses, yards, and parked cars. Marina's heart beats so loudly she can barely hear the traffic that mesmerizes her as she walks to sit on a bench. She must gather her courage. She has no idea of where to begin. Marina knows she will not stay on the streets like her parents did. When they turned 18 and took off on their own, they were as Cook said, "too stupid to find and keep jobs. If we found them, we couldn't keep them. After a while if you can't keep them, you can't find them."

Help is on Marina's mind. God helps those who help themselves, she has read, and she will help and be helped. Before long, she heads to the first yard on a street of confection-colored houses. Marina knocks solidly on the door. No answer. The next. No answer, and on and on until at the sixth house, Marina hears footsteps. A woman peers through the pane.

"Go away from here! Go on. There's nothing here for you."

"I can do work!"

"Not here."

It is at the eleventh house—a large sprawling house with a yard full of toys, that a woman sticks her head out the back door and says, "You can't walk through these yards like this. My neighbor just called me about you."

"I want to have a job. I want to help, have a job. Clean a house maybe." This is a job that Rose had done.

"Not looking like that you don't. Nobody's going to let you in. Don't waste your time. Go somewhere and clean yourself up." She leans halfway out the door, looking down at Marina at the foot of the steps. "Are you okay? How old are you?"

Marina is confused. Weak. She nods, stares at the woman.

"Go clean yourself up. Wait here a minute." The woman closes the door. Marina waits, looking at the blue aboveground pool, the slide, the swings, and colorful plastic balls and tubes she has seen in Wagner's variety store circulars. She is startled when the woman swings the door open and hands Marina two dollars and a fist full of coins.

Grateful for this first help, Marina is encouraged. "Where can I clean myself?" she asks looking down at the money in her hand. It's the first she has ever held that belongs to her.

But Cook has taught her to count money using the crumbled bills and change from his pockets.

"Gas station maybe? Try it. The closest one is two blocks up. That way." She points. "Turn right two blocks up. Get yourself something to eat."

Two people pass Marina on her way—a man and a woman. She asks each one if she is going the way of the gas station. They nod and stare at her without looking directly at her. She stares openly, wanting to absorb their images—so different from Cook and Rose. And three dimensional—unlike her magazine pictures.

"What drug you in?" the boy sitting under the Sterling Filling Station sign says as Marina approaches him. "What happened to you?"

"Can I wash here? I need to clean myself."

"You got that right." He is sitting on a metal chair. Marina recognizes the baggy jeans, the large shirt, the athletic footwear. She has seen boys just like him in magazines.

"Can I clean up here?"

"Yeah. Sure." He ducks inside the station, grabs a key. "How old are you?"

"Thirteen."

"You run away?"

"No," she says and accepts the key.

"Yeah you did." He looks her up and down. "It's around the side."

It takes Marina a long time to open the door, and a much longer time to wash. She tears a strip and rubs a corner of the blanket across a small cake of soap. The faucet is tricky, and she has to hold the knob to keep the water running. She wedges her head into the sink and washes her hair as best she can. She rubs the soapy blanket across her teeth, swishes the acrid solution around in her mouth, then rinses. When she is done, she is standing in a wide, muddy puddle. She dries herself with a dry portion of the blanket, then slips on the dress she has brought along. It is clean and loose.

Marina examines herself in the mirror in a way she has never done before. For the first time, what she sees in the mirror matters. She sees a round face the color of an oak leaf. She has a spray of reddened insect bites. Her hair, pulled off her face and plaited into a wet braid on top of her head, is sunburned to the color of old pumpkins. Her teeth are small and have spaces between them. Her neck is thin, as are her shoulders. Below that, she can't see.

"Better," the gas boy says when she returns the key. "You want chips or candy or something?"

He motions for Marina to make a selection.

"You pick," Marina says and watches as he retrieves candy and chips.

"My treat," he says.

Marina stands and eats. She tastes nothing. Her brain is formulating questions, interpreting sounds, working hard to keep herself upright in spite of the alarming tension that mounts as her minutes at this safe place draw to a close.

"Where you headed?" He buys her a Coke from the machine.

"I don't know. I want to contact government agencies," she says quickly, checking his face for a reaction.

"Government agencies? What are you, a spy?" he laughs lightly. "What kind of agencies?"

"The kind that helps children."

"Want me to call the cops? They'll hook you up with something."

Images present themselves. Images from Cook's words. Uniforms, guns, investigations. "No. Not the cops." She picks up her sack of belongings.

"Okay, good luck. If you need to clean up, come by. I'm here every day till six. No weekends. We're closed."

Marina starts to cry when she turns away from the boy and the station. She ignores her tears. By the time she knocks on the next door, her face is dry.

She has no luck, although she has embraced the boy's words like a charm. Either no one answers, or she is chased away. After a time, the streets and houses fill with children. Their laughter, their words, their gestures, and games are mesmerizing. Marina hides in a yard thick with shrubs and hedges. She watches. She watches roller-skating, ice cream eating, running games. She thinks of Jacob and Boyd. When girls her own age pass by in clothes so bright with color, so new, so perfect, Marina feels swollen with envy, regret, and anticipation.

Everywhere she sees possibilities.

When the streets begin to empty, Marina rises and returns to her search for work. This time, most of her knocks are answered, but either the doors don't open and she is rejected, or they slam quickly in her face. One man says in a thunderous voice, "If you know what's good for you, you'll get the hell out of this neighborhood. You got two seconds to get off my porch and out of my sight."

With this threat, Marina flies through the night. When she slows, there is no light left in the sky. There are no stores—just street after street of houses, each one like the next. Finally, Marina notices a dark and different house surrounded by dense foliage. She turns into the yard, rolls herself in the blanket and rests.

Throughout the night, Marina's dreams and her wakeful moments blend—blurring the edges of reality. The flat, hard ground feels natural and safe. The night sky creates a ceiling for her. Cook, Rose, Jacob, Boyd, and Marina have slept under the stars so many nights. Hot nights when the air in the trailer is like a quilt of steam. The night sounds of birds and insects are soothing, and an occasional song from passing cars rides the wind towards her. But the sounds of people's voices passing by raise bumps on her skin. Rose has told her of strangers using her and leaving her for trash. Cook has talked about film flams and hypocrisy. Their stories fill Marina's head, and she hopes that she won't find anything they've told her about.

A slamming door, mingled voices, and footsteps awaken Marina. Her body tenses and she is as still as death. It is day.

"I just looked out and saw it there, and I wasn't about to go near it and…" a voice says approaching her.

"Well, we got a couple of calls about some kid messing around in some of the yards. We cruised but came up empty."

Marina peers beneath a lifted corner of the blanket. She is totally covered. Two policemen and an old woman—gray-haired and soft—stand over her. Marina prays a frantic prayer in her head, wordless and intense.

A policeman touches Marina lightly with his foot. "Hey!"

The woman reaches down and touches her, jostles her. "Hello."

Slowly, Marina peels back the blanket.

"We won't hurt you," the woman says.

"Show me your hands," a policeman says.

Marina does.

"Jesus," the cop says. "You run away?"

Marina shakes her head, rises. Her head is spinning, spinning, fear, hunger, fear. Inside she screams.

"Where are your folks?"

"Folks?" her voice whispers.

"Parents?"

"I don't have parents," she says quickly.

"Every runaway says they don't have parents. Paul, check for any reports of runaways."

She looks from one to the other. The towering policeman with his voice of stone makes her want to escape from the guilt of her lie. The woman and the other policeman, however, have something different. The man—his face covered with stubble, his eyes the color of pennies, turns her lie into the truth. "I'm not a runaway. I don't have parents. I don't have anything. Nobody."

"You want something to eat? I'll get her something to eat," the woman says. "Can't hurt, right? You're here," she says to the policeman.

"We'll pick something up," says the man with penny eyes. "We'll take her in. That all you got?" he asks Marina, nudging his chin towards her sack.

Marina nods, and understands that she's leaving with these men. With the authorities.

"What's your name? How old are you?"

"Marianne. I'm fifteen." In a daze Marina walks alongside the two men. They open the door and let her into the automobile. A blue automobile the color of a stormy sky. The seat is comfortable. Marina sits back and feels her body straining both against and toward all that is happening. She could explode from the circus of sensations.

"Do you have any family? Aunts, grandparents?"

"No," Marina says. "I have no one." When the words come out, Marina hears them as if someone has delivered the news. She hears them and knows that it is so. That they all left this world when they moved to live among the trees. Their lives ended as abruptly as a novel. Marina remembers Cook's words, "You're nobody out there. You have no number. Without a number in their world, you don't exist." Marina knows this will save her. In the minutes it takes to cross the bridge and cruise through the streets to their destination, Marina buries Cook, Rose, Jacob, and Boyd in deep graves, then walks into an architecturally-perfect building of glass and chrome.

The lady is much prettier than Marina had imagined an authority would be. She wears earrings and lipstick and smells of flowers. Through her fear, Marina can taste a bit of relief. She feels saliva return to her dry mouth. Feels her throat opening. A person, not a figure in uniform, will help her. Marina and the police officer sit down in a short row of connected chairs. Marina watches the lady take out a fresh pad and a fat ink pen. Her heart flutters. Marina sits on her hands.

"I'm Janet Williams, and you are?" she asks, and holds her pen ready to write.

"I'm Marianne."

"Marianne? M-a-r-i-a-n-n-e or m-a-r-y a-n-n?" Janet Williams asks.

"The first one. One name all together," Marina chooses.

Janet Williams writes the name then looks up from her desk. "And a last name?" She turns her head to the side and asks. The woman looks up and meets Marina's eyes, waiting. Marina can think of no name. She covers her mouth with her hand—returning Janet Williams' gaze. Marina's mind skips about, but lights on nothing. Then the woman reaches down below her desk and brings out a tin of candies. Chocolates. Lethal confections. She holds them out to Marina. Marina attempts to hide a smile.

The candy is so sweet that it brings tears to her eyes. Marina is distracted by the tastes blending in her mouth. She is hungry. The policeman did not pick something up as he'd told the woman he would. *I am Marianne*, she says in her mind, convinced by this experience with the box of chocolate in front of her. *I am fifteen years old and my name is Marianne. Marianne. Marianne. Marianne. Marianne.* She says the name to herself again and again and reaches for another chocolate.

"And the last name Miss," Janet Williams says tilting her head in the other direction.

"I don't know my last name. I know I have one because everybody has one. I traveled in a car for a while with my mom and dad. I don't know where we were. It wasn't near here. We drove for a long time. That was a long time ago. I don't remember anything. Only that my name is Marianne."

Janet Williams says nothing. She looks at Marina for a while, then over at the policeman who shrugs. Janet Williams then scribbles on a paper. The room is silent. Janet Williams is deep in thought, then she pulls a book from her desk and flips through pages. The hands move imperceptibly around the clock. Marina hears talk and laughter off a ways. Janet Williams writes and writes, then she tells the policeman she can take it from here. He leaves.

Suddenly, when Marina feels that she is asleep with her eyes open, Janet Williams says, "You come out here and wait on the sofa. I'll be back. Don't leave. If you need anything, ask the lady right outside the door."

Marina nods. She takes in the pale green walls, two large pictures of flowers, a case of books. She wants to cross the room and examine the books, but a knot of fear keeps her glued to the sofa. She thinks of Cook teaching her to read when she was six years old. She picked it up so quickly that Rose said, "I can't read as good as she does. Is that normal?" Marina twists and stretches, trying to read their titles. Through the window she sees only another building—close and taller than the one she is in. Skyscrapers.

After nearly 30 minutes, Janet Williams returns and says, "I have a place to take you. You can stay there for the time being—until we figure out what's what with you, Miss Marianne. Amnesia, huh?"

Marina nods and waits for directions.

"It's going to be a long day for you Marianne. I'm processing you for foster placement. You ever been in foster care before?" Janet Williams asks.

"No. It means a ward of the State, doesn't it?"

Janet Williams' mouth twitches. "Aren't you the little dictionary?"

The day is as long as Janet Williams promised. Marina sits on wooden benches, travels down hallways, and up and down in the elevator. The small room that moves up and down is disturbing to her as it lifts her stomach. Marina waits in hard plastic chairs, then goes through double doors into a room filled with adults and children, desks and more chairs, a corner filled with toys for little children.

Marina is whisked into a cold, white room. She can barely pay attention when a woman doctor examines her—prodding her body with metal and her mind with questions. Marina is rigid with fear. Finally a woman with a tag hanging around her neck arrives. She waits for Marina to dress, then takes Marina across the street to have her fingerprinted. Marina looks repeatedly at the stained fingers.

When the sun goes down, Janet Williams shows up and drives her for nearly an hour. The car is a Ford Taurus. It is white and on the side is a sign that reads "Children's Protective Services."

Janet Williams pulls in front of a two-story house that is painted a dull gray. There is a large porch and nearly a dozen rocking chairs are lined up as if they were expecting lots of company. Janet Williams leads Marina up the walk and rings the bell. "The Braswells are nice people. Very nice people. Treat them right, okay? You don't know how lucky you are that they have a bed," she says.

Marina nods. She thinks of Cook and his warnings. She is filled with pride. She's going to sleep in the house with nice people. A big beautiful house with bushes in the yard as thick as a forest.

Janet Williams stands just inside the door when Mrs. Braswell invites them in. She hands Marina a card, saying "This is your caseworker. Call her if you have any concerns at all. Don't cause the Braswells any trouble. Just call your caseworker the minute you have a question. You understand?"

Marina nods.

Mrs. Braswell says, "We won't have any trouble."

Marina takes in the full fleshy face of the woman in whose house she'll be sleeping. Mrs. Braswell wears jeans and Y-shaped rubber shoes that slip between her toes.

She looks older than Rose, but her smile makes her look younger. Mrs. Braswell closes the door and leads Marina to a large kitchen. She prepares a bowl of cereal for Marina before leading her to the bed. Sugar Pops and milk.

Cook has told Marina that when his mother left, she took the heart out of him. For him there was no family without his mother that he missed so badly. And once there was no mother to tell him what to do, there was no one that he cared to listen to. Not to the teachers who pretended nothing had changed in his life. Not to his father who had too many children and too much on his plate. Certainly not to his siblings which was only a case of the blind leading the blind. So Cook decided to go his own way.

Marina feels she is actually finding her heart when Mrs. Braswell shows her the clean bed smelling of spring. It is the lower bed, a bunk, Mrs. Braswell calls it. In the room are three other girls looking across and down at her with unsmiling eyes. Marina smiles anyway. Nobody will take a sprig of this happiness, this "good luck" that the gas station boy has wished her. The room is so bright. A fresh towel rests on the bed for her. Marina smiles again at the girls who seem unable to take their eyes away from her. One girl laughs. Instinctively Marina feels the ill will lacing the sound.

Marina looks at the girl—pondering for a moment. She is unmoved. Without registering the thought, Marina remembers the strength of her arms and legs—chiseled and muscled from pulling herself into the tops of trees to see more of the world, from swinging the ax to cut down an endless number of small trees to make fires for warmth and hot water. Her senses are as sharp as any jungle predator's from avoiding lynx, wild dogs, and snakes. And most of all, she is unmoved by the prospect of loneliness. She has been lonely for as long as she can remember. Finally, she is in a place that might lead to something other than death. If she is fifteen years old in the eyes of this new world, in three years, she will make the life she wants.

When the light is turned off, Marina closes her eyes and rests well, cloaked safely in her lie. She does not worry about Cook and Rose going to the police or any other authority. They have lived their lives in ways that have removed them from this place and all the places like it. Marina does not know if this is the town that Cook comes to for supplies. If she sees him, she will meet his eyes. She imagines he will spit on the ground beside her—letting her know she has betrayed him. She will love him because he is her father, but he will never take her back.

Sometimes out of nowhere, Cook would call his own father a misguided dick—a slave to his lower self. His mother, Sophia, he called an aberration of nature. "Human parents don't leave their young," he'd say. But lying in bed that night, Marina gives her grandmother, Sophia, a face. It is strikingly similar to her own. But she gives Sophia long, slender legs that glide across great distances. She gives Sophia wide eyes that see clearly where she is headed. Marina goes to sleep comforted by Sophia's courage to go after a life that was calling her—even if her family wept when she turned her back on them.

# KURT—2008

Kurt took full responsibility for Katrina's actions. If he had been home more, if he had acknowledged her loneliness, if he wasn't driving across two states all the damned time, then none of this would've happened. So even though he was the one who'd been cheated on and mistreated, Kurt had meant the "till death do us part." Katrina and the kids were at the center of his life, and without them, he didn't quite know who the hell he was.

Straight out of college, in 2002, Kurt moved to New York and stayed with his oldest brother Boyd. Kurt was likeable. No matter the age or color, people liked his fast southern talk that seemed always to have a bright side. And he was quick. He moved fast, and thought circles around his peers, but still he was a salt-of-the-earth kind of guy. Within three days of starting his job search, Hudson Utilities, a private company serving ninety corporations in a two-hundred-mile radius, hired Kurt as a field supervisor. "There's a lot of driving, and some long hours. You can think, plus you can go under the hood and tell the transmission from the radiator. That's more than we get from most college boys," was what the area manager said when he shook Kurt's hand, and offered him $46,000 to start training the following week.

Kurt called Aunt Edna from his cell phone to share his good fortune. She'd seen him through college—the moves in and out of dorm rooms, the holiday breaks, summer jobs, and finally, graduation. As he chatted with his aunt on the walk from the subway, a young woman walked ahead of him. He couldn't take his eyes off her boy-short haircut, her jeans as tight as stockings, and sneakers—pink like cotton candy. "I'll call you back Aunt Edna," Kurt said, and in two long strides caught up to the girl. "My name is Kurt, and I'm admiring you."

"Oh really?" she narrowed her eyes.

"Yup. I'm admiring you, and I want to ask your name."

"I'm Katrina."

"Katrina. I like that. Katrina, can I please get your phone number. I'd like to take you out sometimes. Get to know you." He stared into onyx eyes glinting like coal.

Katrina said, "Give me your phone."

Kurt surrendered it, and with nails the color of her sneakers, she tapped her number into his cell.

Then Katrina said, "I'm hungry right now."

"You want to go out now?"

"Sure. I wouldn't mind getting something to eat with you. It's public. How dangerous can you be?" Her lips curled into a smile that promised a good time.

"Oh, you're safe. I'm a harmless country boy," Kurt smiled.

"Where'd you like to go?"

"Chuck and Spuds. My favorite. We can walk."

So on the same day he got hired, he found his woman. That same night Katrina dubbed him C.B. for country boy, and had been calling him that ever since. One week in New York and Kurt felt he was on a roll.

It turned out Katrina lived right up the block. As Kurt walked her home that evening, Boyd and Nadina were sitting on the bench outside their two-family house.

"I want you to meet my new friend Katrina," Kurt said. "This is my brother and sister-in-law, Boyd and Nadina. The ones I was telling you about."

"Hi. I see you all the time. I live in the apartment building on the corner," Katrina said, open and confident.

"Hello. I see you, but I never knew your name," Nadina said.

Boyd nodded at the young girl.

After walking Katrina home and kissing her cautiously on the cheek—making no moves toward her lips, Kurt went home. He was sleeping in Boyd and Nadina's finished basement. When Kurt unlocked the front door, Boyd stuck his head out of his first floor apartment and motioned for Kurt to come inside. Boyd said he had seen Katrina sitting on too many stoops and hanging around the bodegas a little too often. "Did she tell you about her baby?" Boyd asked.

"Her baby? What baby?"

"She had a baby about two or three years ago. She had it for four, five months, maybe six months, then the baby disappeared. She didn't keep it till it was walking. A baby in a stroller. Nobody said anything about the baby dying."

Nadina, sitting at the table with a cup of coffee, nodded, confirming Boyd's information; the three of them were silent, giving Kurt a moment to reflect.

Then Boyd said, "I don't think she's much good. As young as she is, I've seen her drinking beer on the corner with anybody. Kind of a street girl. What kind of girl as young as she is can drink and hang out the way she does? And give her baby away, and all the while living home with her family. That's what I wonder."

But Kurt had no interest in such news about the most delicious woman he'd ever met. Plus, he thought of his sister Carlene. On face value people in Haden thought she was careless and unruly. But Kurt knew she was 1,000 times smarter than the people who judged her. They didn't know what to make of Carlene's independence, her having her own mind. So Kurt dismissed Boyd's overprotection, and accepted it as love. Kurt loved love. While others might scorn concern, warnings, and advice, Kurt didn't. What others condemned as nosiness, he accepted as love. What others found intrusive, he welcomed as love. So he smiled at Boyd and said, "She's sweet is what she is. And ain't everybody a street girl 'round here? 'Cause I ain't seen no dirt roads."

Kurt and Katrina were together every evening after his long days of training, and most of the weekend. They sat in parks sipping a beer as they watched games of pick up basketball. They ate greasy chicken and fries out of paper bags; or they took the IRT to the city to eat Chinese, Ray's pizza, or BBQs. Sometimes she met him at the job, and they'd hop on the train and head to the movies. Katrina had lived in the neighborhood for four or five years, and she spoke to lots of people on the street. Kurt knew nobody and was busy working most of the time. So they spent most of their time alone. They never visited or sat around with either of their families. They rang each other's doorbells and met on the sidewalk. Her city savvy and his country curiosity blended perfectly in their own little world. Late at night, Kurt took her to his basement room and she'd stay until just before dawn—just before Boyd or Nadina were up for work.

After a while Kurt did ask about her baby—once he was certain he loved her. Unless he loved her, it wasn't his business. Once it was love, all questions were game. Katrina told Kurt about her daughter, Leah. Leah lived with her great aunt.

"Why don't you have her?" he asked.

"'Because I don't have the money to take care of her. There's no room in our apartment for one more human being if they want to breathe air. My aunt can give her what she needs. And Leah's dad is no help. We weren't married, so he doesn't give a shit. And you can't get money from somebody who has none. I took him to court, and they said he'll have to give me some when he gets some. What sense does that make?"

"But you love your little girl?"

"What kind of question is that? Of course I love her." She shoved him. "I see her. I go and see her all the time. When I leave work." Katrina worked part-time at Off Track Betting. The money was okay. She liked the hours.

"You wish you had her with you?" Boyd asked, leaning in to kiss the hollow valley beneath her neck and shoulder blade.

"Of course I do." She rubbed his head, inched closer to him in the single bed.

"I'll marry you," he'd said, and traced a finger across her brow, past the cheekbones, and down to her pointed chin, so delicate. "I'll be her father."

"You want to be my husband?" she asked.

"I most definitely want to be your husband. I want you for my wife." Kurt felt so full he might explode. His heart was swollen. His sex was bursting. He rolled over and kissed her from her neck to her knees. He pleasured her between her legs. He breathed in the scent of her and wanted to press into her forever. "Will you marry me?" He kissed her sand-colored cheeks, the blue-lined lids, the black satin lashes.

A tiny smile danced at Katrina's lips, and tears glistened at the corners of her eyes. "You really want to marry me?"

"I want to marry you. I want to take care of you and Leah. I want to plant babies in your belly." He spread light kisses where they would be planted.

Katrina giggled. "I would love to be your wife. I want us to be a family." She sat on top of him, like a child, and pressed her palms to her face.

Two months later they went to the justice of the peace. Boyd and Nadina, and Katrina's friend, Miranda, stood as witnesses. The couple found a spacious apartment in an eight-family house in East Flatbush.

Five years and three kids later—including Leah, the couple officially joined the ranks of the unhappily married. Kurt was only 28, but he had the digestion of a sixty year old. Kurt hadn't wanted to separate. He'd wanted to work things out. He offered to find a job with shorter hours, although he loved the one he had. They could go out more often on his days off—just the two of them. Maybe go on vacation without the kids. "We can start over," Kurt promised—anxious to redo and undo the parts that he'd gotten wrong.

"C.B., I'm just not happy. I want to move on."

"Let's talk to somebody, get counseling. That's why they have them. A guy on my job is doing it. Him and his wife. The benefits pay for it. Families need to stay together. That's why they pay for it."

"That doesn't work. I know what I feel. I can't do it anymore. C.B., we're just different. We thought it would work. It's not. You're not happy either."

"Who says I'm not happy? Why the hell wouldn't I be happy?"

"Because we're not even thirty and I can't feel the passion."

Kurt felt a kick in his stomach. He wanted to say, *I can feel it.*

"No. Uhn uhn. We were so young. Too young to get married. We should have been enjoying ourselves in life. Kids get over stuff. My parents divorced. I got over it. Your parents were separated."

"But I don't want that for our kids. They're ours." He went to the cabinet and drank liquid Maalox straight from the bottle.

"It's not healthy to be so unhappy. I want you to find your own place. I'll find one for you if you want. I know you don't have the time."

"I can find my own place if I wanted one, but I don't want one, Katrina." Kurt felt like crying, but he wouldn't. He stood dry-faced and serious like a man, but inside, he was collapsing. He was being pulled under. He sat down at the kitchen table.

"C.B., it's over. I'm not trying to hurt you, but it has to happen. I want you to leave." Katrina went to the refrigerator and took out a bottle of water. "I really want you to go." She took a long drink and turned away from him. She pressed her hand to her forehead and rubbed away tension, then said, "I'm seeing somebody." She glanced toward the narrow curtainless window as she said it.

Kurt couldn't look at her. He turned his back to her and focused on breathing. What he thought was: *How can you say that to someone who loves you this much?*

"You're never home. You never want to party. When you're home you just want to stay around the house. Watch a movie. Play cards. Go down to the playground. I'm sorry, but I want a life." She looked straight at him, her face smooth and without expression. She swung the refrigerator door open and grabbed another bottle.

All Kurt could say was, "How the hell do you tell me you're already seeing somebody when you never even told me what you wanted? You never even told me you weren't happy."

"I don't want to be married. Okay? I don't. I want to think about what I want to do with my life."

"You should have done that before you had a family of four. When you have three children, you already decided what you want to do with your life. You can add on to that, but that's something you're already doing." His voice went low and weak. He felt he might pass out.

"Everybody's not the same."

"Then I'll take the kids so you can figure that out," Kurt said. He rubbed his face hard with both hands.

"You're not taking my kids. I'm their mother. I want you to leave. I said I don't want to be married. I didn't say I don't want to be a mother."

"You were a mother when I met you, but you didn't have your kid." Kurt walked out the door. Later that night he came back, filled a duffel bag, then checked into the Travelers Inn. That would give him time to figure out what to do. But he learned pretty quick there was no figuring out; there was just responding to what Katrina did and didn't do. That became his life.

Five months of separation passed in a series of blinks. As Kurt drove hundreds of miles each week—monitoring his sites and preparing reports, his mind whirred and dovetailed. Kurt found an apartment twenty minutes away. The kids—Leah, Nina, and Bobby stayed over on his days off, and he cooked and washed, and diapered, and potty trained. There was never rest, and he didn't have time to think deeply, or drop down into self-pity. His mind was like a tracking device—just trying to keep up with what came next. He was always in and out of the truck—running to teller machines, stopping at the grocers because the kids were coming that night, using a pay phone because his cell got no reception in a particular zone. He was always calling to talk to the kids when they got home from school, arranging for their visits on his rotating days off. It terrified Kurt that they might question his love for them. His heart propelled him to love them as if they'd all be dead by sundown.

But sometimes Katrina wouldn't take Kurt's calls.

"Stop calling about every little thing. You think I'm retarded? Enough already C.B. We're separated." She changed her cell phone number, so the house number was his only access.

"Of course I'm calling about every little thing. They're my children!" he would strain himself not to yell, because if his voice went negative, Katrina's finger was at the ready. Click.

Then one day, Kurt dialed the number on his way to north Jersey at a time he knew they'd all be in—just after school, before they went out to do anything else. But nobody answered. It went to voice mail over and over again. He wasn't alarmed at first because maybe they were out doing something, anything. But at some point, they should be home. It was a school night, and where do you take three kids when they have to be up at 6 a.m.? So from evening into the night, Kurt dialed and redialed like an obsessed teenager. He completed a form, then dialed the number. Ate a sandwich, then dialed the number. Talked to a customer, then dialed the number. Watched ten minutes of news, then dialed, and so on.

Each time he expected to hear Leah's voice, because she always answered the house phone. Leah, at nine, had become Katrina's stand in when needed. She watched the little ones, made sandwiches, changed the baby. So Leah appointed herself the family reporter—keeping Kurt abreast of what needed knowing. You're supposed to pick us up at 9 instead of 8 on Thursday. Mom had a party last night. Bobby's sick. Nina lost her first tooth. Mommy's out with her friend. I'm sleeping over at Regina's. Mom's spending the night at Miranda's. Mommy made us all go to bed at seven. Blow-by-blow updates. Kurt sometimes wished she'd spare him the details because he could read between the lines that Leah was too young to recognize. He itched to ask more questions, but knew he'd only confuse her, or disturb her—straining her child-woman's brain to contemplate darkness too deep for her innocent soul.

The next day was a repeat of the previous. Kurt was up at Delaware Water Gap at a commercial farm. His reception was in and out, and the company walkie-talkie wouldn't access anyone out of the network. All day he drank Maalox and worried. That night, back in the city, Kurt called the phone company. Katrina's number was working just fine.

On the third day, he repeated the dial and redial process. Nothing. That evening, on his way back to the city, Kurt drove the company truck straight to Rockaway Parkway. He took the stairs two at a time. The door was padlocked. His stomach churned like old plumbing. Kurt gobbled Maalox tabs as he tore down the stairs to question the one neighbor, Mrs. Walters, who knew everything. She either sat in a folding chair in front of the apartment building, or sat guard on her first floor window seat. Kurt found her in the window.

Mrs. Walters gave Kurt just enough information to turn his nerves into spaghetti. "I didn't see them leave, but I've been away. I took my spring vacation to my daughter's house in Riverhead. Nice place in Riverhead. Nobody's said anything to me about your family since I got back. I got back Sunday, so whatever happened must have happened at night. They must have left at night. But I haven't seen them at all."

Mrs. Walters craned her neck out the window to investigate a crying baby, then she turned back to Kurt. "Young man, I tell you this for your own good. For your family's good. You need to get your children away from that crazy woman tonight. Get them away." She enunciated each word separately and firmly. "I don't know how long it's been since I've seen her sober. Her head is in a cloud somewhere. In the clouds. And I don't want to upset you, but you came to me. You came to me. So I owe you the truth, wouldn't you say?"

"Yes m'am. I want the truth. I appreciate anything you can tell me. I'm very worried about my kids. And my wife. Her too." Kurt wanted to cry. He felt helpless and alone.

"Well. Another thing. I don't like the man she's with. I don't like him. He's creepy. And he drives like a maniac." Mrs. Walters frowned and shook her head. "Get your children."

"I don't know where she is. I don't know where they are." Kurt stood in front of the building and looked up and down the street. He knew he wouldn't see them coming.

What he saw was a glimpse into his own past. Maybe his mother had been right to leave them with his father. All his life he had thought about the mother he missed. He'd loved his father in a begrudging way because Hunt was all Kurt had. But Kurt never knew the straight story about what happened between his parents before Natalie and Charles came into the picture. If Kurt didn't find his children, they would always wonder what happened to him. That was all mixed up in his mind as he stood there questioning who his own mother was—wondering for the first time if he had always been better off without her. Things looked so unfamiliar and so uncertain from where he stood. He felt dropped into a puzzle and didn't know where to begin.

Kurt took out his phone and stared at it. He dialed his brother Boyd. "I don't know where the hell they went or what happened. Do me a favor and go by Katrina's sister's house. Her name is Lucy Roman. Just introduce yourself. Tell her who you are, and you're trying to help me 'cause I'm worried about the kids. The address is 876 Kilcullen. You can tell her to call me on the cell."

"You got the sister's number?" Boyd asked.

"It's not working. Boyd, call me and tell me what you find out. If you can't get me, keep trying. I might be out of range. I need another cell company is what I need. But keep trying. And Boyd, thanks a lot. I know Katrina's not," Kurt let the thought drop. Boyd would look out for his family. No matter how he felt about Kurt's wife.

"Don't worry. I'll let you know."

Kurt then drove ten minutes to check with Miranda, Katrina's friend. Miranda was half-dressed and getting ready for work when he knocked on the door.

"Hey C.B.? You never come by me. Everything alright?"

"I'm looking for Katrina and the kids? You seen them? Or heard from them? It looks like they got put out of the apartment."

"Put out? She didn't pay the rent?"

"That's what I'm figuring. But I gave her the money. There's a padlock on the door. I put money in the account for it every month."

"Well, she must have did something else with the money. You checked the money's not in the bank?"

"Yeah I checked. The money's gone. Where the hell do you think she could be?"

"She told you she was seeing somebody right? Cause she told me she told you." Miranda looked at him from the side, and quickly turned away.

"She told me."

"She's probably staying with him. Maybe."

"Her and the kids?" Kurt's hairs stood on the back of his neck. Just the idea of his children in another man's house.

"Could be. I would think so. Maybe. Last time I saw her, she said she was going over to Donnie's for a couple of days. She didn't say she was going to stay or anything. She didn't say moving in. C.B., you want a beer, a soda?"

"No thanks. Donnie? That's his name?"

"Yeah. I gotta finish dressing. Keep talking. I can hear you." She went back into her bedroom raising her voice.

"Well, where the hell does this Donnie stay?"

"I'm not sure."

"Miranda, I really need to see what's going on with my kids. You understand that. Finding a padlock on the door and not knowing what happened. That's not good."

"No. It's not. But I don't know where he lives. In Bed Stuy somewhere, but I don't know exactly. And C.B, I don't want you to start shit with him. You're too good. He's not the kind of person to start shit with."

"What the hell does that mean?"

"Nothing. Really. I just don't want you screwing yourself up over somebody like him."

"Somebody like him? What the hell is wrong with him?"

"I don't know what he's into. I just know he doesn't work. And he's not broke. That's all I know. He lives somewhere off Grand. That's all I know."

Kurt had never felt this kind of tension. His head was tight and his breath squeezed through his windpipe, as if he'd run for miles, uphill, in steel boots. He punched Maalox from the blistered card and chewed. "How stupid can she be? What the hell is going on in her head?"

"I don't know. I tried to call her a couple of nights ago, but her cell's going straight to voicemail."

"Well she blocked me from her cell. I couldn't get to her anyway."

"That's really a shame. I feel bad C.B. I do."

It was nearing 9:30 p.m. Miranda left the house with Kurt. He dropped her at the subway, so she could make it to her job by 11. Kurt was high-strung and frantic—still talking through the window as Miranda waved and walked down into the station. They would keep in touch.

His next move would be the police. He didn't know what else to do. Just as Kurt pulled onto the highway, his cell phone rang.

"I'd like to speak with Kurtis Sawyer," a woman's voice said.

"Speaking."

"Mr. Sawyer, my name is Ms. Little. I work with children's services."

"Yes m'am."

"I have information about your children. Do I have the right Mr. Sawyer?"

"I have three children I'm trying to locate right this minute. Is that the one you're looking for. God I hope so."

"Yes. We have your children. But you'll have to come into our office in the morning for more information."

"Can I come tonight? Are they alright?"

"They're doing well in light of what's going on. Do you have a pen to write down the address for our office?"

"One minute please. Let me pull over." He pulled to the curb and took information about the appointment for 9 a.m. She told him to bring identification—one with a picture, and his proof of address.

As Kurt hung up, Boyd called back. "What's up Kurt?"

"I just got some information," Kurt replied.

"Good, cause her sister hasn't lived there in a couple of months. They moved, but nobody knew where."

"Thanks Boyd. I think I've found them. At least the kids. I don't have the details, but I'll let you know what happened tomorrow morning."

Kurt was on the steps before the doors were unlocked. He was jittery from little sleep and too much coffee. He felt like he was hovering outside his body. These days seemed to be happening to somebody other than the man he was. He'd tried so hard to be somebody that a wife wouldn't leave. Then he tried to be the kind of father that children wouldn't doubt. There was nothing he knew to do differently. It cracked him to his core.

There were pages of forms and hours of waiting on first a hardwood bench, then an orange plastic umbrella chair, and finally on a cretonne sofa before Kurt saw the social worker, Ms. Little, who was authorized to tell him about his family. A drug trafficking report led the police to Katrina's apartment. Drugs were found on both Katrina and her male codefendant, and there were more drugs found in her bedroom. Ms. Little wasn't at liberty to say who the man was.

She said, "I've been informed that it might be a while before bail is set, so we're uncertain about the chances of your wife's release. The courts are backed up. You've probably heard it on the news, that trying drug cases is a priority right now—and they are proceeding so carefully so nothing is missed. Too many mistrials."

Kurt nodded. Already his insides were straining and knotting, and his stomach was on fire. He was following along as patiently as he could, scared for his wife, waiting for the part about his children.

"And I understand you and Mrs. Sawyer are separated."

"Yes m'am."

"Since you were separated, I'm assuming you knew nothing about what was happening."

"No m'am. Not at all. I don't have anything to do with drugs."

"That's good to hear. As for the children, they were taken into protective custody because there were drugs in the apartment. They're in an emergency placement until we get through this process. We tried to reach you the evening of the arrest, but we didn't get through, and," Ms. Little paused and rubbed her temples, "well, the wheels start turning, and we have protocol, and this is, unfortunately, how long it takes to follow it. It's cumbersome. But the children are safe."

"When can I get them?"

"As soon as we run your background check, and confirm that you don't have any warrants or child abuse records. The reports are actually running right now. I'm not going to find anything on you, am I? You aren't wasting our time, are you?"

"No m'am. Absolutely not. I don't even have traffic tickets. How long?"

"Depending on our Neanderthal technology, in a little over an hour you can go and pick them up." Ms. Little put down her pen and looked straight into Kurt's eyes. "Mr. Sawyer, this is what I want to say to you, the father. Your ex-wife or wife, however you refer to her, has made bad choices. Your children had nothing to do with that, and yet they have to go through a very, very hard time because of her choices. You are what they have. You are the person who can bring some stability into their lives, and get them past this trauma—because it is a trauma. But I'll tell you what I see more often than I'd like. The mother or father gets custody of the children. They proceed to drop the children off with this one or that one, while they get all wrapped up in helping the husband or wife who made the bad choice. They act as if the bad thing has actually happened to the criminal. That is a travesty. So hear me, Mr. Sawyer."

"Yes m'am."

"The court system will give your wife the attention she needs, through lawyers and hearings, and the legal process. She and her codefendant involved themselves with drugs. Adults know drugs are illegal. The courts can unravel who did what and so forth. You leave this office and give your children your attention. The last thing an intelligent man such as yourself will want to see down the road is your children getting locked up for making bad choices. And you know why most children make bad choices Mr. Sawyer?"

Kurt shook his head. He was wound too tight to search for such answers.

"Because their parents made bad choices. So I'm asking you to make good choices when it comes to these children."

"I hear you, m'am. I'll take care of them. I have what I need to take care of them. I know what to do." And Kurt felt like he did. He knew what it was to be left. He thanked Ms. Little as he walked through the door, and he thought about all she said as he drove carefully down Eastern Parkway through Crown Heights into East New York. He found the address—a turn-of-the-century walk up. The foster mother called Leah, Nina, and Bobby from a back bedroom. When they came out looking small and scared, Kurt wouldn't let his mind dwell on the fact that his wife—the woman he'd planned on loving forever, was in jail. He tried not to think at all.

Kurt believed in neighbors because he'd grown up without a mother. Where others might have checked and double-checked and picked a person apart, Kurt trusted his instincts. A friendly face and a reliable "good morning" was usually enough to get on his good side. Now Kurt had three children to raise, and he needed help. For the rest of that week and all of the next, Kurt used vacation days and took the children everywhere with him—so afraid they would be terrified without him. They clung and laughed and cried so much more intensely than he remembered.

He arranged for school buses and an after school program for Leah and Nina. He approached an older, retired couple in his building about watching Bobby who was only two years old. The couple declined. "Our health wouldn't allow it," the woman said, but she made a recommendation. By the end of the week, Kurt had arranged for the babysitter, and his life was working—hour by hour. Whenever he thought of pursuing Katrina, he heard Ms. Little's voice. He wanted to tell somebody all that had happened, share the details and bare his soul. But what did losing a wife to such a man say about him? How did he choose a woman who preferred a drug dealer? What did it say about her? It mattered to Kurt what people thought about the mother of his children.

Kurt jumped into his role with the precision of a diver. He made fast, simple dinners—hotdogs and baked beans, grilled cheese sandwiches, Spaghettios and corn, whatever he could whip up by 7 p.m. after long days in the field. He played with them, then ran baths, made a bedtime snack, and finally read a story and tucked them in. When Bobby cried, Kurt was quick to pick him up and comfort him, carry him around the apartment if need be. He let all three children fall asleep around him while he dozed in front of a ballgame or the news. Inside he sobbed because he knew they wanted their mother.

Kurt asked his friend Otto from work to come by a few times. Later in the evening to catch a game, have a beer. But the few times Otto came by, Kurt had sat nodding like an old man—exhausted. He was bad company. Nadina and Boyd spelled him a couple of times—but the two youngest cried so much, Kurt didn't have the heart to put any of them through it again. This was the life he had, and he didn't think one way or another about it. But as their lives fell into a rhythm, and they moved beyond triage, Kurt still missed Katrina with the regularity of a heartbeat.

He wanted to do a better job than he thought his father had done. They'd always had food and heat, and decent clothes for school, but Hunt Sawyer was like a shadow. He left early in the morning, before they got up for school; and he came back in the evening, checked to see if the girls had made dinner, then was gone again. Sometimes he didn't check at all; Hunt worked full-time and took side jobs off the books. Time probably got away from him. Plus, Hunt trusted his daughters to hold it together. Kurt knew he could do it better because he knew what it would feel like if he didn't.

One evening at the end of the summer, when Kurt's family was in the chaos of bath time, the phone rang. Kurt, with a half-dried Bobby in his arms, answered. It was a recording requesting a collect call from Katrina Sawyer. He accepted the call and felt a prickling heat spread like a rash all over his body.

"C.B.? It's Katrina."

"Wow. Hey. How are you?"

"Hey. You can imagine. I've been better."

"I'm surprised to hear from you." Kurt walked to the back, and diapered Bobby. He had no idea what to say. He had imagined meeting up with her again—once she was out of jail. A phone call had not entered his mind.

"How are the kids?"

"They're good. They're alright. They miss you."

"I miss them. How can I even talk to them since everything that's happened?"

"You just talk to them. What else can you do? Having a mommy in jail is better than having no mommy at all." He envisioned her pink sweaters, sneakers, nails, lips. So much pink. Such a woman. Thoughts raced around in a blur too fast to capture any of the words. She had rejected him. Taken ridiculous chances with another man. Put his children in danger. And still Kurt couldn't locate the anger. Relief was all he could register.

"C.B., I would have called before."

"Yeah. I guess things aren't easy to manage. Jesus."

Katrina talked a bit about how the lawyer filled her in about children's services and his getting custody. How she stopped worrying because he was such a good father. But still, it all happened so fast.

Kurt listened for words that would calm the fears lurking in his entire body.

"Is Leah handling everything? Still being in charge?" Katrina asked, and Kurt could hear the smile in her voice.

"Not so much. You must have given her the courage. She's different without you." Kurt rubbed Bobby's back, soothed him into sleep.

"You're a good father. I know they'll be fine with you."

She had to go quickly. It was late, and they had restrictions. As she was hanging up, Kurt slipped in, "Call me tomorrow."

All day Kurt anticipated the call. Like first-date excitement, Kurt rushed to get through the evening routine, knowing, hoping there was something worth waiting for on the other side. Ten minutes earlier than her call the night before, the phone rang.

This time Kurt had questions. "So how long before you know anything? Is there a trial? What's happening exactly?"

As he asked, Ms. Little's voice echoed in the back of Kurt's mind. He hoped it would all fall in place without violating his agreement.

"Actually, I'm getting out at the end of the month. What happened is I got charged for possession, but I only had a bag of weed on me. There was weed and pills in the apartment in a backpack, but they all belonged to Donnie. And, I'm not saying nothing good about him or anything, but he did tell the lawyer that the bag was his, and I didn't have any knowledge of the other drugs and what he was doing with them. So I got simple possession, no intent to sale."

"Good."

"So they're assigning me to a halfway house in a couple of weeks. They've already scheduled me. I'm waiting for the final processing. I have to go through a rehab program, then do two years probation."

Kurt sat on the edge of the bed holding the phone closely to his ear. "That's great, Katrina. That's good news. I'm glad. So you can see the kids soon?"

"Yeah." She paused. "And you, hopefully."

"So what about Donnie? You guys are, what?"

"Donnie is nothing but the past. Donnie's going to prison. C.B., I screwed up. Even if he wasn't going to prison, he would be nothing to me. Having all this time to think, I know I've been stupid. So damned stupid. I just got caught up in a lot of craziness for nothing."

Kurt had nothing to say. The pain of betrayal quickened, and he listened intently to hear beneath her words.

"Donnie's nobody to me. You can't imagine how many tears I shed for losing everything for nothing. I got tired of being mommy all the time is all. I took a distraction." She paused, but Kurt did not fill the silence. She continued. "I should have just went back to work. If I had been smart, I would have just got a job and put the kids in daycare."

Kurt heard it and felt space enough to share an opinion. "That would have been better. Yeah. For sure." Even if they didn't work out, it felt good to know Katrina didn't love somebody else. He breathed deep, closed his eyes. "So at least you're getting cleared, kind of. I mean you'll have a record, but at least you don't have to serve a lot of time."

"That's the bright side. I've served enough time already. This is not...Let's just say it's horrible. It's horrible. When I walk out this door, you better believe I will not be back."

"So does being in the halfway house mean the kids can see you?"

"Yeah. I can go out. It's not like total jail. I just have to check out, say where I'm going, be in at a certain time, like that. I'll look for a job, and I can give them your address, so it will be okay that I come and see the kids. If it's okay with you."

"Of course it's okay. That's good to hear. It'll be good to see you."

"Really? I'm surprised to hear you say that. But I'm glad. I am really sorry for hurting you C.B. You can't know how ashamed and sorry I feel for doing this to my husband."

"Well. Yeah. It hurt. It really hurt." Kurt wiped his nose on the wet towel beside him on the sofa. The regret and pain connected Kurt and Katrina through the phone lines. Then suddenly they were in a new space—beyond the gaping wound, when the blood has darkened and there is a promise of healing. Kurt said what he had been wanting to share with her for weeks. "Bobby's talking."

"No? He was saying nothing. Like three words. That's it."

"Overnight. One day he said, 'I don't like this milk,' and he never stopped talking." He smiled to hear her reaction. It felt good to talk about his children. Every detail that had happened to them flooded into his mind to tell her. He'd been so lonely without his wife. She was the only person who cared about all the things he wanted to say. How could a parent leave that behind? How could they go off into the world knowing a part of them was learning something new, or crying themselves to sleep, or losing their teeth without her? Wouldn't their tiny broken hearts haunt her soul like demons? Kurt wondered if Sophia's soul had allowed her any rest at all.

Within two weeks, they would come together as a family for the first time in nearly a year. Kurt didn't know what he would do, what he would have to change to make his marriage work. But he would find out because—short of her death, his children would never lose their mother again. No matter what. Kurt walked through the apartment checking the doors and windows. He looked in on the children. In the morning he would tell them Mommy was coming back. He shook his head. He couldn't believe his good fortune.

## BOYD AND LISA—2010

Boyd was invited to sit at the head of the table. The cavernous room and a wooden chair made him feel like he was about to be punished. But it had been a long time since Boyd had done anything wrong—like splattering gasoline near a group of teenagers in front of the senior citizens' building. He had run them off holding a box of grilling matches ready for strike. Or like slashing the tires of that electrician for taking his aunt-in-law's money and not finishing the job. Too many heavy-handed points had been made along the line. But now Boyd was in his forties; time had taught him to turn away from acts that jeopardized the life he had with the people he loved.

He was in the judge's chamber with four state and county representatives and a stenographer. There had been some mention of who they were and where they were from, but he had no recollection. Boyd was a straightforward man. If he was just giving what he had—no more and no less, it didn't matter who they were.

"Tell us what you think is important for us to know. Asking a set of stock questions just generates a set of stock answers. You tell me what you think is important for making a decision." That was the judge's instruction. Boyd took a deep breath, looked off to the side, and started with where he was. He would work his way backwards and sideways—however it was called for to make the points worth making.

Boyd started with how his life was changed six months earlier. Jilstons had given him the option of taking a buy-out or relocating to China; it was a no-brainer. It wasn't like he was a scientist or a doctor pulling in big money. Nothing to make it worth his while to endure the discomfort of calling a strange land his home. He was a welder by trade. So on the day Jilstons deposited the buy-out money into his account, Boyd turned the sum over in his head and knew exactly what he would do with it.

Neither he nor his wife, Nadina, were big spenders. A little comfort was about all they craved. And there were no children needing tuition funds or future weddings to worry over, so they had saved plenty over the years. Many wondered why the couple, so solid and easy-going, had no children. Though they had none, children had come through their home at various times. Early in their marriage Nadina's baby nephews had stayed long enough for people to think they belonged to them. But eighteen months later, their father came for them. Another time Boyd's sister, Carlene, had left her daughter with them while she did a three-year stint in the army. And just three years ago, Boyd's niece, Fallon, Eva's child, had shown up as dirty and wiry as a spider monkey. Her parents wouldn't sign for her to get married. The teen had run away with the boyfriend, but somehow or other, they got separated. She made her way to Boyd's upstate New York address—right outside of Peekskill. They kept Fallon for three weeks, long enough to brainwash her back in love with her own family. They drove her back to North Carolina. Boyd and Nadina were always listed. Throughout the Sawyer family, Boyd was the just-in-case brother and uncle; Nadina was the same—the fallback sister and aunt.

Everyday for a month, Boyd called his bank to hear the mechanical voice stating his buy-out balance. That was long enough for him to finalize his decision. Boyd drove 76 miles north to meet a guy from Craigslist concerning two singlewide mobile homes. He had already prepared the land behind his house—nine acres all together. Two weeks after that, he bought two more. Three weeks later, nine mobile homes were within eyesight of Boyd and Nadina's kitchen window. He had $48,000 worth of used mobile homes that would double or triple in value once he refurbished them. But Boyd wasn't making a trailer park, nor did he have a trailer-flipping plan. He was making a commune.

He had thought about communes since he was in his twenties, right after he met a woman named Alexis Hart. At that time, he was just old enough to realize he and his siblings had something akin to afflictions that started with their mother's leaving. They'd had Sophia just long enough to probably go on missing her forever—each one in a different way. When she disappeared, Boyd had already moved into a house with two of his friends. So he was already gone. But being so close to the suffering she left behind was unbearable. It was hard to watch seven kids scrambling to make do, and his father making it all up as he went along. Boyd could do next to nothing for them, and having a cloud following him around was no way to live. Plus, that's what a person did: left home. It wasn't his place to raise his siblings or worry his own life away. They had Hunt for that. So within the year after Sophia left, Boyd took the bus to New York and started working.

So one night, a few years after he'd been living in Brooklyn, Boyd and some coworkers went across the street to have a few beers. Next to him was a young woman playing the jukebox, singing along, chatting up the bartender and anybody else within earshot.

"So, you live around here?" she asked Boyd.
"I work across the street. I live in Brooklyn."

"That's too bad. I just moved up the street. I'm looking for neighbors. I'm kind of a people person. What's your name?"

So they struck up a conversation that pretty much focused on why she was such a people person. Alexis Hart said, "I grew up on a commune."

Boyd's interest was piqued. He rarely talked to anybody who'd done anything outside any box he knew about. He questioned her.

She explained. "I had like 12 mothers and nine dads, and like 50 brothers and sisters, so people were just everywhere, all the time, so I don't feel normal if I'm by myself too long. I haven't seen anything like it since I left. And I left 11 years ago. It started out with six friends—my mom and dad were among the six. And they bought a house in the country, fixed it up. They weren't ready to spend a lot of money on rent and mortgages. They were kind of hippies at heart. So it started with them sort of living the way college kids do— only they had adult lives. Jobs and bills. Then kids started coming and they expanded—buying prefab houses, putting a mobile home here and there."

She continued, "There was always someone to love me. Even if somebody was pissed off at me, or didn't want to be bothered, there was somebody who did. And what I think worked too, is that some of the adults went to work on real jobs, but some worked around the homes—fixing stuff, cooking, growing veggies, watching the kids. It worked. Looking back, everybody seemed satisfied. More content than I see most people being in their lives—married or otherwise."

By the time she and Boyd turned back to their own drinks, he understood that communes were more than hippie love and what he'd seen on television. When she said it made her feel secure and very loved, Boyd had listened with a sharper ear. Over the years, he would remember that evening. And he'd think about how different things would have been for the youngest of his siblings. He could barely think of them without having a leaking feeling around his heart.

So when Boyd bought those mobile homes, he was tending to a seed planted 15 years earlier. In random moments, he imagined running into Alexis Hart. To credit her with giving him a vision he never would have come up with on his own.

Boyd cleared his throat, adjusted himself in the seat. He had never been called upon to just keep talking without any back and forth. He paused. Nobody said anything. The judge nodded for Boyd to continue.

Once he got into renovating the trailers, his sister Lisa came to his mind over and over again. It was like some kind of message that wouldn't go away. Without prior intention, Boyd reserved the best mobile home for Lisa and her kids. He started scrubbing corners and cabinets with some special disinfectant Nadina brought home from the hospital pharmacy. When Lisa and the kids visited, Boyd hoped they'd overlook the fact that he was suggesting they trade a brick split-level in Forest Hills for little more than a hut. But Boyd thought it was important. He was committed.

So one evening in August, Boyd was dead tired. He leaned against the fence and watched the sun making its way towards Bear Mountain—daydreaming. On impulse, he took out his cell phone and dialed Lisa's number, like he often did.

They had the usual back and forth: How are you? Good, and you? The kids? Nadina?

Boyd had taken a long listening breath before he went on. Hopefully she was alone. Lisa had a way of maneuvering in and out of relationships pretty fast, so he was glad to hear silence—no evidence of a companion. With Lisa, you had to work quick because she could fall in love quicker than you'd start feeding a stray cat.

So Boyd and Lisa talked on about how much her real estate sales were bringing in—even in this economy, is how she had put it. But that wasn't surprising because Lisa was smart when it came to books and learning. But her true talent, with men and women, was a kind of play-acting that she learned way too early for her own good. Lisa would look deep into people's eyes, acting like such important words had never passed anyone's lips. This talent not only rented and sold property; it kept her getting in and out of hellish, quicksandy relationships that were hard for an older brother to watch. Sometimes it took months or years for Lisa to disentangle herself from a man with enough baggage to take a cruise for the rest of his natural life. One of the recent ones was swimming in gambling debt, and Lisa made the mistake of lending him money. The last one Boyd met had such a strong tendency toward women and men that Boyd was scared to be alone in a room with him, for fear he would hurt the man.

Lisa was still young, had enough money to have a good time, and she was kind of wild. Boyd understood that. It took all kinds. He was no saint. But what made him so uneasy was that she had married three times. Each marriage produced a child: Jerry, Mae, and the youngest—Fernando Jr.—called Fuzzy. And to make it worse, which gave Boyd a bit of heartburn, was she was still married to Fuzzy's father—Fernando Cruz Sr. Fernando Cruz harbored a religious streak he wasn't trying to hide. Lisa would catch him sprinkling holy water around the front of her house any time of the night or day. And one weekend Fernando had a rosary tattooed on Fuzzy's bicep. Fuzzy came home with a reddened, swollen crucifix and brown beads peppered down his tiny arms. In his overnight bag were directions to apply A&D ointment until further notice. This same man, from some small Central American island, did not believe in divorce and would not sign the papers. He wanted Fuzzy to have married parents until he was a grown man. Lisa had long since moved on, and fallen in love at least twice more. As if she was not still legally Mrs. Fernando Cruz.

Boyd hated to even think about Lisa, but she popped up in his mind all the time. Probably because for 16 years, she'd lived close by—no more than an hour or two away. Boyd was a person to fix things. That's what he did. And Lisa always had something to fix.

So that August night when Boyd called his sister, his agenda became to sell her on his vision. Because she either didn't have one, or it involved going around in circles that led to nothing but more circles. He could keep an eye on her, protect her, if she was in the back yard. Boyd said, "Lisa, it's shaping up like I planned it. You never really think about actual dreams coming true. Good things happen in life, but the big dreams pretty much remain fantasies. I'm having my fantasy!" Boyd had laughed out loud. He couldn't keep his excitement in check as he explained how he'd planted both fescue and shade grass, how a community garden would make people think more about what they ate. Two displaced Jilstons women would offer childcare services for little children. His voice had gone low and serious when he said, "Lisa, it's going to be a place where people won't have to work so hard to be happy."

"It sounds wonderful. Staying happy is like an actual job. Boyd, if you can make that happen, you may actually be in the miracles business. I'm not kidding." That was Lisa's response.

Boyd was hopeful. "I'm glad you said that because I've fixed up a place for you and the kids. I know you have a life already, and you're not looking for me to come up with a plan for you, but I know things get kind of stressful sometimes."

"Yeah they do, but no, I'm not…" Lisa's voice trailed off.

"I know, but it's something to consider."

"Thanks. I think. You're setting something up for just me? How about Carlene or Eva, or Kurt and Katrina? Are they getting reeled in too?"

"For now, just you. You're my city sister. You've got my city nephews and niece. I worry about them. I don't worry about the others as much."

"Boyd, I'm pulling into my driveway now. So let me get everybody settled. I'm happy things are shaping up. But you know, I don't think your commune is for me. I already have too many people in my life." She laughed. "Don't you think?"

It cut him a little bit. Not hurt exactly, but it didn't sit right with him. He loved all his siblings. He was the oldest. He had seen each one crawl, then walk, then talk, then move on to suffer in his or her own way once Sophia left. But only Lisa had that fast-moving-train thing about her. Half a dozen times in the last three months, she'd dropped off the kids in the middle of the night—literally. Each time she called when she was five minutes away, "Can you guys watch the kids?" Each time Boyd broke into a sweat—scared something was happening to her. He was always mentally preparing to respond in whatever way was necessary—because it seemed like just a matter of time. Maybe Fernando was chasing her down again like he had a couple of months ago—angry she was eating at a restaurant outside with a man. She'd driven to a police station and parked so he would get off her tail. He'd done it again as she was riding a client around.

But fortunately, these middle-of-the night drop-offs were just party opportunities. Boyd and Nadina would stand by as Lisa settled the kids in the spare room. They didn't mind watching them. But neither Boyd nor Nadina liked the idea of Lisa traipsing through the night on deserted highways with kids who should be sleeping. Mae had complained about it. "I hate getting up in the dark. I'm too tired the next day," is what the girl said. Boyd mentioned it. Lisa dismissed it.

Weeks would go by and all seemed fine, then there'd be a call from Jerry after midnight on a school night: "Did my mom call?" or a random question: "Did Mom tell you Fernando came in the movie while we were there?" Then Boyd would start worrying and getting a headache. Have to take an Excedrin. Powerless was not a position Boyd was comfortable with.

Whenever Boyd took the drive to North Carolina to visit the other sisters, he felt even and steady along the way. First he'd stop in Haden to see Carlene. Her husband, Jermaine, not the strongest brick in the foundation, looked to Carlene to lead them through a simple enough life. He worked at a chicken factory some ways off—and was proud of his back porch icebox filled with the benefits of such a job. He would fry vats of chicken and make a tub of slaw and entertain when Boyd and Nadina were in town. Carlene and Jermaine had renovated the Sawyer house, and Carlene had turned their old shelter into a structure slightly bigger than a shed. She painted it black and hung a sign: Capture That Tattoos. It did good business. One visit Carlene had tattooed a jagged hacksaw along Boyd's forearm that matched her own. "It's sort of a pun," she'd giggled. A hustler by nature, Carlene was also charging people, on a sliding scale, to do paperwork. Carlene said, "When I got in the army, I found out school hadn't taught people a whole bunch of stuff they really needed to know." That was her opportunity. She filled out people's papers for everything from mortgage applications, to bank loans, to job applications, to medical forms. She'd put on her jeans and Frye boots with a pressed white blouse and show up with her "client" just like she was their lawyer—ready to read the fine print and fill in the lines in her careful handwriting. Boyd once watched her get ready to go on one of her appointments. He'd been very proud of her.

Next he would stop and see Eva. And Eva never changed. She was always smoking cigarettes—never the same brand,

and thin as a razor. But Eva loved her children with a fervor that gave her a solid view of the world. That kept her in a forward-moving state of mind. Her life was a series of little hurdles—somebody needing braces, going up to see the teacher, a quirky asthma condition, suspicious rashes, Fallon's young marriage. And Eva still had Dan—always a phone call away, and sometimes a short- or long-term visitor. "I don't have the stomach for love. Love would just do me in for good," Eva confessed one evening, sitting on the porch of the old farmhouse. It was situated on a two-acre strip in front of a commercial farm. Boyd felt Eva belonged in the life she had.

Boyd saw his younger brother, Kurt, pretty often. And Kurt's heart was wide open. His wife, Katrina, was definitely the kind of woman who might break it two or three times. Now and then Boyd itched to pull Katrina aside and remind her of what she had. "Don't take somebody that solid for granted; especially not somebody with a kind heart to go along with it," is what Boyd would say. But Kurt was a man. He had skills, he loved his wife, and he tried hard to do what was right. Boyd chose to believe that Kurt had gone through enough hard times already. Fate couldn't be cruel enough to continue to punish such a good man.

The other brother, Cook, was a mystery. Too many nights of gasping awake in a sweat taught Boyd to cast thoughts about Cook and Sophia out of his mind. Not knowing if people you loved were dead or alive was its own kind of living hell. When watching the news—especially reports of murders and bodies turning up—Boyd would sometimes brush the edge of a breakdown—where tears collected in his chest and burned like heated oil. But Boyd would snap off the TV and get up quick. Find something to do.

Boyd propped his elbow on the table and rested his head in his hand for a second.

"You're doing fine," one of the women at the table said. "I hate that you have to go through this, but the only way to really know a person is to hear from him—first hand. You're doing fine, Mr. Sawyer. Hang in there."

Boyd nodded, poured a glass of water from the sweating pitcher on the sleek polished table. He drank it down. He shook his head. Life spun on a dime and everything changed—just like that. Like sitting in this room, with a fresh haircut, in a tight brown suit, spilling his guts so strangers could decide his fate.

"Since nobody's perfect, could you talk a bit about a situation you feel changed your life—maybe a mistake you learned from. A life lesson, so to speak," the judge said.

Boyd lived with a kind of superstition; the things worth hiding were the things that somehow came to light and did you in. So Boyd told the story of the Thursday night when he was 31. The Four Corners Bar and Grill was the place he stopped in to have a few beers before and after work. He was working the second shift—four ten-hour days with perpetual three-day weekends. And for him and his buddies, Thursdays were payday and party nights. Sometimes a few drinks turned into enough to make the night disappear altogether. But this particular Thursday night would be the start of a bender that lasted twenty-four days. It left him in a totally different state than when he started it. It must have been some one-of-a-kind full moon. The last thing Boyd remembered was slipping quarters into the jukebox. The rest was a tarred strip laid over his memory. When he came to, he was in his apartment on the kitchen floor. There was an eviction notice under his door; his hair was matted with blood, and he was wearing only one shoe. Seemed like he'd been in a fight. A deep, dull pain throbbed on his right side. First thing he did was call his job. "Mr. Ruffin, this is Boyd."

Mr. Ruffin said, "What the hell is wrong with you?"

"I'm hurt." Boyd touched his side, confirming that there was, indeed, a pain in his body.

"What do you think I'm stupid? Don't call here after you've had your drunken holiday down in the bar."

Boyd strained to remember the days past, but none came. He waited stupidly on the line, hoping for something.

"Listen Sawyer. If you need me to tell somebody you're a good worker, I'll do that much 'cause that's the truth. But that's it."

"I can't come back?"

"You can't come back. I already filed the papers. AWOL. Good luck, Sawyer." Click.

During the three and a half weeks, Boyd had managed to lose his job and his apartment. Through calls to his buddies, Boyd pieced together the nonsense that accompanied a bender—which meant nothing at all, except that he had been out of control. Boyd regained his life a bit at a time: staying at the YMCA, searching the classified want ads, drinking coffee by the quart. He swore he'd never drink again. Within a month's time, he found the job at Jilstons that he would keep for 13 years. Four months later, he'd met Nadina.

"I started drinking early," Boyd told the judge. "By the time I lost my job and apartment, I'd had enough of drinking anyway. Never had so much as a sip since that day I woke up in my kitchen."

"Do you understand why you drank so much?" the judge asked. "Why you started drinking so early?"

"I think it's just what some people did. My father's social life centered around going out and drinking. We didn't have a happy home, so I guess drinking made sense as a pastime. Turned into a habit." Boyd's thoughts turned briefly to the year when he learned to drink beer and liquor at Breezy's, one of Haden's liquor houses. When Boyd was sixteen, he'd often sat at the back of the paneled room in a wooden booth with his friends. Leon was eighteen, and he bought the liquor they all shared openly. More often than not, Boyd's father, Hunt, would stop in on his way to wherever he was headed. Boyd would hear Hunt talking with his friends, and his father's voice took a tone they never heard at home. Talking serious about the job, stuff in the news, prices. A part of Boyd took pleasure from knowing the man as none of his siblings did. And Hunt did not chastise Boyd for under-aged drinking in a bar. Now and then, he would walk over and set a beer in front of his son. Hunt would pluck Boyd, knock off his cap, or touch his shoulder. Their closest bond was made away from the house that would eventually break all their hearts.

One night Hunt came into Breezy's with a woman. Once they were in the room, the two separated and pretended not to be together. But Boyd saw the moment when Hunt bought two drinks and handed one to the woman who happened to come through the screen door two steps behind his father. Half-hour later, Hunt bought two more drinks and did the same. Boyd was hot, and he got hotter with each sign of their lie. Without even thinking, Boyd strode across the room to Hunt and looked him in the eye. "Give me your money. I'm taking it home," Boyd said.

Hunt reared back on his heels and looked at his son. "Give you my money?" he asked in a voice suggesting a joke had been made.

"I don't want you spending Ma's money on another woman," Boyd countered, using all of his will to keep his voice from shaking.

Hunt had studied him for a long moment, perhaps considering what to do in a situation he could never have anticipated. But then he reached into his pocket, pulled out his wallet, removed his bills. He handed them all over to Boyd except one. "I'm keeping a ten. Put the rest in the back of my bottom drawer—underneath the undershirts." Hunt watched Boyd put the money in his pocket. "You're a good man, Boyd," Hunt said. He put his arm around Boyd's shoulder and squeezed it before releasing him into the room. But Boyd didn't go back to the booth. He went straight home and did as his father had told him.

He loved his father. Even 18 years after Hunt's death, a place inside Boyd could recall the exact feel of his hands, the smell of his work clothes, the faint air of stale whiskey on his weekend breath. That night at Breezy's changed things. He wished he hadn't seen his father and that woman. After that Boyd walked through the world with different expectations—way more likely to keep both eyes open. Now he wondered if he could ever keep his eyes open wide enough. Boyd looked down, tightened his fists beneath the table. Was there any truth to the notion of having a handle on something? You thought things were under control, and the next minute you found you're on a waxed marble slope with your feet flying up in the air.

Boyd wiped beads of sweat from his forehead, slipped his thumb in the base of his collar to make some room. God almighty. Boyd breathed deep—took a minute to pull himself together. He cleared his throat, shifted around a bit more, brought his mind back to the task at hand. There was a time to let go, and this wasn't it. At a time like this, the judge needed to know what he was bringing to the table. What kind of insights. Boyd would let them know how all his sobriety and superstition had developed his sixth sense. And how the twists and turns in Nadina's life had done the same for her. That together, they had a momentum going— a strong momentum in the right direction.

Boyd's venture could have gone one of two ways: become a commune or turn into a trailer park. Either way there was the same up front process of wiring and installation: septic systems, water lines, plumbing. A spiral notebook sat on the counter tracking service people, agency contacts, docket numbers and such. Boyd was never idle. He was on the phone or swinging a hammer, or tightening screws, welding rods, or ripping out or installing paneling. The day started at dawn, and it ended when the energy was totally spent. Jeff and Benjamin, his closest friends, both bought out from Jilstons, worked alongside Boyd like he was paying wages. But all they got was a heavy meal at the end of the day and access to the refrigerator full of lunchmeat, sodas, water, and beer. Day after day, the men showed up before Nadina left for the pharmacy. They knocked at the back door, came in and drank the pot of Mr. Coffee before picking up where they'd left off. Week after week, trailer-by-trailer, the weathered mobile homes were transformed into decent, nice-looking dwellings.

First, one of Boyd's former coworkers, and then another, inquired about moving in. A friend of Nadina's sister was interested. Word of mouth traveled fast. By the end of September, all but one of the trailers was fully renovated, and six of the nine were occupied. Benjamin, after the months of steady labor, fell in love with the land where trees were scattered just far enough apart to feel the sun without roasting. He wanted to settle in the immaculate rectangular living quarters that didn't cost an arm and a leg. So Benjamin decided to leave his Mount Vernon apartment and move his wife and sons to a place he helped to create. That tipped the scales in the direction of commune. It was a place where people cared, and wanted to become part of a community—a family.

A while back, with most of the hard work behind them, Boyd and Nadina went to eat at the diner on US 6. With the windows down, an east wind blew the smell of Peekskill Bay through the car. Nadina talked about finally starting her herb garden. She had gone to pharmacy school for a while, but life happened, and she never got licensed like she planned. The commune gave her a potential clientele for homegrown healing—bruised children, nauseated mothers-to-be, men and women with arthritis, asthma, chronic indigestion, frazzled nervous systems. They discussed the patch of land to till for such a purpose. They listed what they'd need: soil, manure, vermiculite, blood meal, lime. Then out of blue, Nadina asked, "Wouldn't it be good if we could get Lisa here?"

"Why do you ask?" Boyd had not mentioned his holding the home aside for his sister. "You must be psychic."

"I didn't like the way Fuzzy and Mae looked last time we were in the city. Jerry's old enough to fend for himself. But the little ones will grow up to be crazy. The whole time we were there, Lisa was on the stoop screaming on the phone."

"She was a mess. I have to admit it."

"Yeah. And the kids were a wreck too. They pick up her energy. If she's nervous, they're nervous. That day, all Fuzzy and Mae could do was watch her, and Mae's chewing her nails like they're friggin candy. I'll speak honestly. Lisa has nothing left for those kids."

Boyd had to agree. The past year she was out of control. Maybe it was trying to keep her life the way it had always been and stay one step ahead of Fernando. The level of emotion was off the charts—and still Lisa kept moving all the time. She seemed never to sleep. She was doing anything at any time—like she was living around the clock.

Nadina brought up one thing after another. "Remember last time when she stayed for the weekend? She was on the phone all night, and came down in the morning looking like the kiss of death with the baby dangling like a rag. She'd probably kept him awake with her yapping. She had big circles under her eyes, and she put the baby down, and said, 'I have to go. I'll be back.' Then that friggin maniac shows up. Of course you remember."

Of course Boyd remembered. Ten minutes after Lisa said she had to go, she was dressed up and gone. Ten minutes after that Fernando rang the bell. Boyd answered and treated him as decent as he could treat a man who tracked his sister's movements like it was his job. Boyd offered him a seat. Legally he was still his brother-in-law. It was the least he could do in front of Fernando's son and stepchildren. Fuzzy was glad to see him. Boyd noted how Fernando's eyes slid slowly from one corner of the room to another, up the stairs, peering around and under things. He detected a few quick prayers. Boyd was uneasy, so he remained standing.

"I hear you have a lot of time on your hands lately," Boyd said.

"What do you mean?" Fernando asked.

"I mean, Lisa and the kids say you show up any time, any place, out of the blue. You out of work?"

"No. Of course not. I have a son to support."

"It's a very flexible job you have that lets you track them like that. Is that normal?" Boyd asked.

"I'm not tracking anybody. I have a good schedule. Of course I love my family, but I'm not tracking."

"That's good. "Because I don't think tracking is normal. Might not even be legal," Boyd said.

Fernando asked to be pardoned for stopping by so unexpectedly and leaving so soon.

"No problem," Boyd had said as he escorted him to the door. Boyd reminded himself to tell Lisa that it was not a good idea going to meet her lover with a husband so wrapped up in her comings and goings. That judging from the vibe he got from Fernando, she'd do better to figure out how to get that divorce. Boyd mentioned it to Lisa.

Lisa replied, "Fernando can do whatever he wants to do. And I'm a grown woman. I can do what I want."

"You're what Fernando wants to do," Boyd told her. Lisa had chuckled.

So Boyd's last-ditch effort to reel Lisa in was Thanksgiving. When he invited her for dinner, Lisa said, "Thank God. One of the dads is always trying to break us up for the holidays—trying to take his kid, like we don't all want to spend it together. So I end up telling these magnificent lies just so we don't go off in every direction. Now I can tell the truth and be done with it. I'll tell them my big brother wants us all there together this year. Count us in."

It was as much a housewarming as it was Thanksgiving dinner. Boyd had cleared out the two-car garage and lined it with tables. He had invited the whole Jilstons crowd so they could see what was going on.

By noon, a pig was basted and roasting. Two turkey fryers were sizzling. Some folks were sitting around on tree stumps, buckets, and boulders either cooking or just enjoying the process. The atmosphere was buzzing with success. Some of the men and women had no job prospects, and a few had taken lower-paying jobs than they had before. But there was a richness in the air that many had never felt before. Boyd bathed in it as he walked from the woods back to the house to fill up a half-gallon thermos with coffee.

He looked up and caught a glimpse of Lisa's son, Jerry, playing among the other children. Already he had fallen into a ballgame with the kids in the field. When Boyd and Jerry made eye contact, the boy tossed the ball to the kid nearest him. "Uncle Boyd!" he called and half ran to meet him.

Boyd choked up, but didn't quite know why. Perhaps it was the thinness; or the faint shadow of manhood on Jerry's upper lip; or because Jerry looked so much like Boyd's brother, Cook. Boyd grabbed the boy and swung him in the air, pulled him into a hug and didn't let him go for a long time. The bond between them shot through Boyd as powerful and painful as a toothache. In that moment, he wanted so much more for his nephew: more stability, more time just being a kid, more running and playing outdoors, more time away from his mother's slipshod life and the men latched onto her. "I'm glad you made it."

"Me too," Jerry responded. "I like the place." He kept pace with Boyd as they approached the house.

"Good. I hope you'll spend a lot of time here. You see there's plenty of kids. Already making friends, huh?"

Everybody had come together to bake, chop, fry, and simmer everything from the turkey and stuffing, to curried coat, rice and peas, greens, potatoes, casseroles, baked breads, field peas, rice pudding, cakes and pies. Lights were strung from tree to trailer to tree to trailer. If there was such a thing as magic, it was there on the outskirts of Peekskill that Thursday night. Dinner spilled from their dining room, out through the side door into the garage. Nadina arranged for Thanksgiving speeches. She said people were thankful for him, and they were proud of him. As was she. They needed the opportunity to say that. The guys from Jilstons who'd helped out and those who had come to live in the trailers brimmed with emotion. It was more than anybody thought it would be—Boyd included. They now understood what a vision was.

Boyd watched Lisa as she worked the room. Charm should have been her middle name. As she talked to different people, she touched them and laughed, and her face was a kaleidoscope—changing from moment to moment to suit the companion's story.

After they'd eaten, Boyd and Lisa sat on the front porch—to catch up, see what came up face-to face that didn't on the phone. It gave Boyd a chance to sell her on the idea. After the festivities, maybe she would recognize some possibilities for this place. Fuzzy and Mae had latched onto a clump of smaller children to hang out with. Mae, Lisa's middle child, was a weird one; she reminded Boyd of an owl. She was a quiet, thickish child with big round eyes and a slow blink. That she fit in warmed Boyd's heart. It was a sign of the commune's healing power. He had a good life— loved his wife, loved this venture, loved the friends he'd collected from one place or another over time. He wanted his sister, and especially her children, to know what it felt like to be satisfied.

Lisa had leaned against the iron banister. Her short spiked hair and shiny makeup made her appear to be glowing in the moonlight. Seeing Lisa at that angle, Boyd knew his commune had nothing to do with a woman like her. She had no need for space and land and these close connections. Changing her location would not extinguish her desire for nightlife, after parties, flashy men, and the drama, as Nadina called it. Lisa wasn't looking for peace anymore than Boyd was looking for a medical degree. Standing there on the porch, he was struck by how off he could be when trying to resolve somebody else's life. He might be scared for her, and he might want better for her children, but he couldn't control Lisa. And this place wasn't the answer for her.

A little before 11 p.m., when the house was clearing, and the dishes were done, Boyd strapped Fuzzy in the car seat, hugged them all, and watched as Lisa drove off.

It was 1:43 a.m. when the phone rang. Boyd automatically looked at the clock on the side of the bed. Nadina answered, and the first thing Boyd heard was crying—hysterical crying. Nadina was saying over and over, "Calm down," as she leaned to hand Boyd the phone.

It was Jerry's voice. Through screaming cries, Boyd heard the stabbing words "shot Mommy." Boyd felt like concrete had slammed against him. "Call the police! Call 9-1-1!"

"I did," Jerry replied. "Now I'm calling you."

Boyd tried to stay calm for the boy. He didn't know anything except he had to get there. The next thing he made out through Jerry's cries was, "took Fuzzy."

"Stay in the house, Jerry. Lock the door and wait for the police. Let the police know your uncle is coming for you. Don't let them take you. Stay in the house." Jerry's cries filled the room. Boyd's own tears came in a flood. He called 9-1-1 himself and repeated what Jerry told him. The minutes after the call were a blur. Everything was sweating. He couldn't remember where he put his keys though he put them the same place everyday. Through gauzy moments, Boyd put one foot in front of the other until he and Nadina were heading south on the Taconic Parkway.

They were quiet on the ride. "No matter what happens, you've done everything you could have ever done for her.

She knows she can count on you," was the only thing Nadina said during the hour-long ride.

Two police cars were parked in front of the house with the lights flashing. Yellow tape marked off the manicured square of yard. If neighbors had come out to see, they were already back inside, and their lights were out. EMS was already gone, and the lights were blazing in the house. Boyd and Nadina navigated their way around and over the tape to get inside. Three police officers stood in the living room. A woman in rough-dried clothes sat on the sofa with Jerry and Mae. As soon as Jerry spied his uncle, he ran across the room, jumped into his arms and buried his face. Mae followed—rushing into Nadina's.

"I got you," Boyd managed—his voice screeching through vocal cords already taut with grief.

"I need to ask you to identify yourself."

"I'm Boyd Sawyer. Lisa's brother." He reached for his wallet to show I.D. They immediately confirmed that Lisa Sawyer Cruz was dead.

The rough-dried woman with horse sense written all over her had already sat mugs of hot chocolate in front of the kids. She got up so Nadina and Boyd could sit on the sofa and squeeze the children between them. She left the room and soon returned with travel cups of black coffee for the adults. Nadina and Boyd accepted them like life rafts.

The older cop explained the pieces Jerry hadn't told them. Shortly after the family returned from Thanksgiving dinner, Fernando Cruz rang the bell. He was shouting through the door that he was going to a convention the next day. He wanted to see Fuzzy before he left—especially since he missed being with him for Thanksgiving. Lisa was yelling at him, asking if he was insane—coming to visit in the middle of the night. Fernando said it was a holiday, and people stayed up on holidays. He had been waiting for hours. Plus Fuzzy was still awake and was talking to

Fernando through the door. Lisa finally let him in. Fuzzy and Fernando sat on the couch. Fuzzy sat in his lap. Lisa went to the kitchen. Jerry and Mae went upstairs to get ready for bed.

Soon after, Jerry heard Lisa screaming at Fernando. "No, you can't take him with you. We're all going to bed. You can pick Fuzzy up next week like we talked about." Jerry came out of his room and sat at the top of the stairs. Fernando told Lisa he was done with her making all the decisions. He got up and carried Fuzzy across the room. Lisa told him it was time for him to leave. He said it was also time to take Fuzzy with him. When Fernando stepped towards the door, Lisa moved to block him. Fernando pushed her aside. She kept her balance and moved in front of the door again. There was pushing and arguing. Fernando pulled out a gun and hit Lisa in the head. In the temple. She fell to the floor. With Fuzzy screaming in his arms, Fernando shot Lisa four times and walked out the door and to his car. The bullets went straight to Lisa's heart and her brain.

Jerry said he was so scared he couldn't move. Mae was shaking and crying beside him. He didn't know if he should go to his mother or call the police. But his mind came to him and Jerry was already dialing 9-1-1 as Fernando was driving away. There was an alert out for Fernando Jr. and a warrant for Fernando Cruz, Sr.'s arrest. Only time would tell.

The wind left Boyd's body. He clung to Jerry and wept silently onto the top of the boy's head. He kept wiping Jerry's head and crying into it again. Jerry was still.

The family was up all night. The woman had a briefcase filled with papers. Several forms and signatures granted permission for Boyd and Nadina to take the children home with them. Temporary custody.

"What about their father?" the caseworker asked.

"There are two fathers: Henry Levy and Gerard Patterson," Boyd explained. "My guess is they'll want visitation, but not custody."

A standard investigation had proven Boyd's guess to be dead on. So the county set up custody hearings. They would determine Boyd and Nadina's fitness to assume primary custody of Jerry and Mae.

In the days that followed, the couple's talk centered almost entirely on raising Lisa's children. It was like they were pregnant. That all their years being childless had been leading them to this task. Preparing for the children gave Boyd something of Lisa's to fix his mind on. All the worrying and planning and desires for her were over. He was afraid of the space she was leaving inside him. Boyd needed to raise these children.

"That's all I can think to tell you," Boyd told the officials around the table. He drank the last of the water in the glass, feeling a bit lighter—knowing this session was coming to an end. "Except," he added, "when my father died, my younger sister Carlene didn't, wouldn't, live with anybody in our family. She was declared independent just before she turned 17 years old. She told me point blank, 'You all won't know how to make me feel any better.' It was a heartbreaking thing for a kid to know so early. So with that, and a lot of other things I've learned over the years, I know I would never let Lisa's children down. I know exactly how to make them feel better. I want the chance to make up for some things that children shouldn't have to go through. When our mother left, I was too young and immature to do anything for the younger ones. I can do something this time." The stenographer typed that in.

They would call Nadina in next. She would sit in the same chair. They would listen and decide if she held the same vision, the same commitment that her husband did. Boyd would have laid down his life that there would be no gaps. He and Nadina were matched that way—in what they wanted, in what they believed.

Boyd shook hands with the people around the table and walked out of the room. There was no doubt that at the end of the day, papers would be in the works—papers declaring him a parent. There would be evidence on record predicting that he would be a good one. That he and his wife were capable of raising children without causing them undue harm.

Boyd thought of his parents. They'd had no such luck.